Fungi Foul Play

VIKKI WALTON

Morewellson, Ltd.

Fungi Foul Play

For permission requests, write to the publisher:
Attention: Permissions Coordinator
Morewellson, Ltd.
P.O. Box 49726
Colorado Springs, Colorado 80949-9726

ISBNs:(e-pub) 978-1-950452-44-6
(standard paperback) 978-1-950452-45-3
(large print) 978-1-950452-46-0

Cover design by DLR Designs
Formatting by Wild Seas Formatting; Rik Hall

CHAPTER ONE

Anne had a strong focus on her phone, her attention completely taken by whatever was on the screen. The phone call went unanswered, as it had many times before. Frustrated, she ended the call.

As Kandi made her way to her SUV, Anne gave her a friendly greeting of "Good Morning." After Kandi had made her way into the vehicle and shut the door, Anne put the vehicle in drive. "Hey, over the past few days, I've been attempting to get in contact with Hope yet I'm still waiting to hear back. Have you been in touch with her and heard anything from her?"

"No, but she's probably preoccupied with all the things she's doing. You should have come to the mushroom class she held at the Herbal Shoppe. It was so interesting! I am counting down the days until I can go out into nature to learn the art of distinguishing and recognizing mushrooms.

They're going to hold a foray next month, I think. You should come with me."

"Um, maybe." Anne's mind was distracted as she drove toward Main Street, her gaze shifting to the left side of the road. "What's with the holdup? Hey, instead of taking the main road, why don't we travel along the back road to get to Polly's place? What has caused the recent surge of traffic in the mornings lately?"

Kandi replied, "Well, for one thing, you barely ever head out in the mornings. And second, with so many people now being able to work remotely, plenty of individuals have moved away from Denver and the other big cities and have ended up here."

Anne let out an exasperated sigh that showed her current state of frustration. "All I can do is hope and pray that they will make their way back soon. We certainly don't need these newcomers here."

Kandi couldn't help but giggle as she remarked, "Of course, it's easier said than done—although it doesn't really apply to you since you yourself are a transplant!"

"I don't think I should be included in that count." Anne gave a knowing wink before engaging her turn signal and then began to turn left down the street towards Polly's Pet Shop.

"What are you getting from Polly again?"

"Some new toys for Mouser and the supplement he needs. I want him to stay around and healthy for a long time now that he's getting older. He's seemed a little out of sorts lately. I took him for a check-up at the vets, but his vitals are all good, so he has no health issues to speak of. But I thought some new toys could be nice."

"Who knew you'd be so wrapped around his little paw?"

"Guilty as charged." Anne let out a heavy sigh. "So much for bypassing the traffic. It looks like everyone else had the same plan of steering away from main street."

Kandi leaned her head closer to the right of the front window, as she squinted past the truck stopped in front of them. This morning she had spent some time styling her hair, which was full and wavy, into two braids. The braid in her hair had been done in a rush, leaving a strand of hair that had fallen over her left eye and cheek.

Anne cracked open the window of the car to let in some of the refreshing air that was typical of Colorado, and while she waited for the line of vehicles in front of her to move, she glanced up at the sky. The sky was filled with fluffy white clouds that drifted on the air. Along with the soft breeze, the remnants of a light rain from earlier in the morning had left dew on the plants and ground, filling the air with the fresh scent of wet grass.

Anne took a deep breath and sighed with contentment. "Ah, that smell is wonderful. I love mountain air."

Kandi murmured her agreement but asking, "Do you ever reuse plastic baggies, because they're still in good condition?"

With a slight tapping of her fingers on the wheel, Anne waited for the truck in front of her to move aside so the other car could pass. "Yes. If it was not too much of a mess, I may just decide to wash them out. Why do you ask?"

"Do you think that they, like, do that with body bags?"

Anne was taken aback with surprise and gasped out the word, "What?" She took a moment before continuing. "Kandi, sometimes I don't know how your mind works. Why in the world are you thinking about that?"

The truck in front of her rapidly turned onto the street, bypassing the car heading in their direction in the other lane. With the truck moving out of the way, it left the road ahead of her completely unobstructed.

Pointing in the direction ahead, Kandi said, "Look!"

About halfway down the street, just before the hilltop, two strong men were carefully placing a black body bag into the coroner's vehicle.

"Oh, my word."

A car's horn honked behind her, forcing her mind back on the road. "Geez, everyone's in a hurry these days."

With Anne steering off the road, Kandi craned her neck to take in the scene before turning her gaze back to the front. "That's a terrible way to start your day, huh?"

"No kidding?" Anne asked skeptically.

"It makes you stop and think, doesn't it? I mean, look at you."

Anne made a face, her brows knitting together in confusion. "What are you trying to say? Why are you looking at me?"

Kandi responded nonchalantly, shrugging her shoulders, and making a downward motion with her hand. "Like…you're in a declining phase now, right?"

"Excuse me? I'm in a 'declining' phase. Seriously? Forties are not even close to a declining phase. In fact, I know people in their sixties and seventies who could out hike you and me because they're physically fit." She huffed.

"No, I know that. I'm just saying you're on your way to fifty, and then next thing you know, eighty."

"You know that's everyone. Even you youngsters in your twenties. The thing is growing older is a gift lots of people don't get to experience. I appreciate every year God gives me on this earth. All that aside, I should not have brought you along today. You aren't doing much to boost my morning morale."

"Ah, you know you love me." She angled her head in her usual gesture, her latest earrings gleaming in the morning light and jingling softly.

"I do love you. But stop calling me old. I'm far from being old." Anne applied pressure to her brakes as the vehicles ahead began to reduce their speed. "Come on, people. What's the hold-up?"

"See, that's what an old person would say." A grin spread across Kandi's face.

"I'm going to throttle you."

"Not until after breakfast, okay? Speaking of breakfast, you got anything in here to snack on?"

"No, I don't have any before breakfast snacks on hand. Sorry," Anne said. She observed Kandi's face and noticed that her cheekbones, which were usually very prominent, had become less defined since she married Stewart. Nothing unusual about that, though. Anne was in the same predicament since Carson had become part of her life. Her recent gain in weight could be attributed to her lack of exercise in the winter months. Once she got back into gardening and working outside, she should be able to get back into shape and drop the extra weight.

Anne couldn't help but smile as her mind dwelled on Carson and the pleasant thoughts he brought. Even though they were so different, they somehow made it work. She noticed a vacant parking space in front of Polly's store and switched on the signal light on her right-hand side in order to stop and park her car.

Polly's was located on the well-known Market Street in Carolan Springs, alongside many other shops. People had established their stores inside of large, Victorian style homes, living on the upper floors while their businesses were conducted below. Nowadays, there are plenty of places to pick up treats for your pets, find stylish clothing and home décor, get a new hairstyle, and enjoy some unique café fare. After they grabbed what they needed from Polly's, Anne and Kandi were planning to head down the street to one of the newest places. The French Bistro was a short walk down the street from Polly's, and Anne and Kandi had planned to head there after picking up their items from her.

"I love how Polly decorates her house all year long." Kandi grinned at the house now decorated in bunny ears and whiskers.

Polly had decorated the house at Halloween and Christmas, but as she saw it grabbed attention for her shop, she'd continued adding to the theme throughout the year.

"Yes, it's fun. But too much work. Though I'm sure it's great for advertising." Anne checked her rearview mirror before exiting the vehicle, slamming the door behind her.

Kandi joined her on the sidewalk, and they made their way up the steps where Polly's newest addition, a rescued Maine Coon cat, sunned himself on the porch's wide railing.

"Hello, Max."

In response, the large, fluffy cat meowed and tilted his head back to receive some ear scratches. "He appears to be in a happy mood today."

Kandi replied, "It's hard to tell what cats are thinking."

"Actually, I think it's pretty easy. Feed me. Pet me. Get away from me." Anne stroked his back for a moment before dropping her hand.

Finally, with a shake of his head as if to signify that he had had enough, he began to groom his paw. Anne opened the screen door wide and motioned for Kandi to go in first.

A bell designed in the shape of a bird was above the door and it chimed. It emitted a who-who like an owl. Anne peered up at it. That's an innovative concept.

Polly yelled from the back room. "Be there in a minute!"

Anne called back. "Take your time. I've come to retrieve my package. We can explore until you're ready."

Kandi went to the section that had bird treats. "I may grab a few of these seed packets for my girls."

Kandi was talking about the chickens she had in her backyard that kept growing in numbers.

Due to the increase in the price of eggs, she had been making a good profit by selling eggs to those around her. Not that Kandi needed the money. She'd come into a substantial inheritance, so she never need worry about money again. And yet, it hadn't changed her and much of it had been placed into funds that would grow for retirement, along with some giving she'd allotted to many charities close to Kandi's heart.

Wiping her hands on a dishtowel, Polly made her way out of the back area. "Apologies for the wait. I've adopted a few more animals and had to finish cleaning up the bowls used for breakfast."

"If you keep going like this, you'll have a zoo in no time." Anne quipped.

"I'm merely helping a friend who's on vacation. I don't believe I'll be adding any more pets to my family."

Anne laughed. "Do you remember saying something about this before you acquired Max?"

With a chuckle, Polly remarked, "That's certainly the truth, but I don't have to take him for a walk like I do my sweet dogs. Even better, his meowing is quite effective, often luring people up onto the porch, and then it's only a few more steps until they can start perusing and buying. I should call this place Max's. Anyway—"

She made her way to a counter that had shelving that went all the way up to the highest point of the ceiling. A ladder that had been constructed to be used for traveling along the length of shelving was fastened at the end. "I'm sorry for the delay in getting this in before now. And would like to express my apologies for it." Her cheeks flushed with color as she exclaimed, "I'm frustrated with constantly reordering the same items! It's starting to cut into my profit big time now. I even have had to go through the process of canceling the delivery to my door, which is an additional step on my part."

"What do you mean?" Anne took the box Polly handed down to her.

"Porch Pirates!" Polly huffed.

"Porch what?"

"It's people who steal packages from porches and doorsteps, commonly referred to as 'porch pirates' ".

Kandi joined them. "I heard of it in bigger cities or suburbs, but not here."

"You're right. We never had this issue in Carolan Springs, but unfortunately it's becoming increasingly more common. I've talked to quite a few business owners and almost all have been hit at one time or another. Sorry, I shouldn't have spouted off like I did. It's just so frustrating."

"No need to apologize. I'd be upset too. I wonder if they're only going after businesses or if they're hitting people's homes as well." Anne replied.

"Not sure, but what I know is that it's gotten worse. A lot of business owners have complained, and we even called and sent emails to the police. But they're sneaky. No one has seen them. Often porch pirates will follow behind trucks and then grab the packages, but this one tends to know when things are showing up. We think it could be someone local."

"But we've never had, like, this problem before." Kandi said.

Anne huffed. "Transplants."

CHAPTER TWO

Kandi rolled her eyes. "Oh gosh, not again with the same old thing…"

Polly chimed in. "All I know is enough is enough. It's got to stop. We used to be where we could leave our doors unlocked and everyone was friendly."

"I guess you could, like, put up a camera." Kandi said.

Polly's eyes narrowed, and she pursed her lips, clarifying that she was not pleased with the suggestion. She then gave a firm shake of her head, emphasizing her disagreement. "It's so depressing. I moved out of the city so I wouldn't have to deal with this. Or to feel the need to put up security cameras."

"So, you don't have a camera?" Anne asked.

"Nope. So far I've refused, but I may have to give up my pride and get one. There has been an increase in people putting up surveillance cameras, though. Who knows? Maybe I can work it so I can also have a Max cam at the same time, though why anyone would want to watch a cat on a video is beyond me."

Kandi laughed, "You can't be serious. People make all kinds of money with their animals. Especially cats with shorts or reels, and meme's."

Polly held up her hand. "I'll stop you right there. I'm one of those strange old fuddy duddy's who doesn't do social media or any of that."

Kandi responded. "I could help you with that."

"Sorry, but my budget comprises paying for the upkeep on this place, feeding my menagerie, and, if I'm lucky, being able to put money in savings for the slower months in the winter."

Kandi was talking animatedly, her face beaming with expectation. "You wouldn't have to pay me, but I've been thinking about starting my own online business and you could be my guinea pig. If you like it, and it brings in business, you could give me a recommendation. What d 'ya say?"

Polly shrugged. "Hmm. Let me think about

it."

"I think I've figured it out," Kandi suddenly exclaimed in an outburst.

Anne pivoted in Kandi's direction, her face filled with curiosity, "What is it you've figured out?"

"I bet I know who's behind the thefts."

Anne stood still with her arms crossed over her chest, patiently awaiting Kandi's next words. "Okay. Who is it?"

"The security companies. Think about it. Stuff gets taken. To discover who's responsible, it's necessary to install cameras. Then, no more thefts."

Polly and Anne's eyes met before they burst out in laughter. "Kandi, I, well, I just don't know what to say."

Kandi crossed her arms. "It could be."

"Yes, but I'm willing to bet that they don't do that."

Polly chimed in. "Well, if they could, I bet the security people would love that idea. Kind of like the broken window theory."

"The what?" Kandi asked.

"Never mind. Anyway, I will think about what you've said. On the social media thing. Now, Anne, your total is thirty-two fifty-five." As Anne dug into her purse, Kandi shuffled off to look at something else that had caught her eye.

Polly took the card Anne handed her. "That kiddo sure has a different way of looking at the world."

"You have no idea. Today she wondered if they re-use body bags."

"Hmm. I've never thought about it. Do they? Oh, crud. Now I'm going to be wondering about that too. You all better find out and let me know!"

"Will do, Polly. Oh, and round up the total for the rescue to thirty-five."

"Great. Thanks."

"How's the new rescue doing?"

Polly swiped Anne's card in the machine before handing it back to her. "Pretty good. We have a quick turnaround for most animals. Hey, doesn't Mouser need a friend?"

Anne took her card and stuck it back into her

wallet. "Absolutely not."

Kandi had returned, her arms laden with items. She faced Anne. "But think of poor Mouser, all alone."

"Mouser is fine." Anne hoisted her purse over her shoulder and waited while Kandi paid for her items.

"Polly?"

"Yes?"

"We saw that someone died this morning over on the Bells. Have you heard anything about who it was or anything else?"

"Ah, this explains the body bag question." Polly took the items from Kandi. "Sorry, no, but my mornings start early, and I haven't even had a chance to finish my now cold coffee." She used her hand to brush her bangs out of her eyes delicately. "Where are you two off to now?"

"We're going to try out the new French bistro at the end of the next block. Sounds like it's good from what I've been hearing."

"It is. The quiche is a great option, however, I find the omelet with asparagus and gruyere cheese to be delicious."

"That sounds wonderful." Anne said.

"It is. You can choose from a croissant or baguette slice, rosemary potatoes, or a salad, as well as a small cup of fresh fruit from the current season. The desserts and pastries you can get to go are absolutely mouth-watering and I could talk about them for hours. If I don't start limiting myself from going there almost daily, I'm going to have to do a lot more hikes in order to keep my pants fitting."

Kandi's stomach growled.

Anne laughed, "I think that's our cue to head off. Thanks again, Polly, and sorry to hear about the porch pirate. Hopefully, they'll be caught soon. Oh, I have my car parked out front. Should I move it?"

Polly shook her head. "No, it's fine. I opened up more space in the back for parking and there's always room on the street."

"Okay, thanks. See you later." Anne waved as they exited onto the porch, where they said their goodbyes to Max before taking the steps down onto the sidewalk.

Anne unlocked her vehicle, putting the package in the backseat's floorboard. Kandi added her items as well. With their packages safely tucked away, they strolled along the large sidewalk, recently added by the city that made this area even more inviting. Trees along the street were budding out with flowers and leaves. If a late spring storm didn't come in and knock off the blooms, the street would have a beautiful display. As they walked down the street, Anne noted that many of the stores still showed the Closed sign in their doors or windows, often opening later in the day and staying open later. During the summers and over the Christmas holidays, stores also stayed open on Thursday evenings to allow for more shopping after people got off work.

They strolled down the sidewalk to the lovely little bistro, once a rock building that housed a hotel and bar. The owners had done a wonderful job of bringing a touch of France to the site with shutters added to the windows and ironwork to the adjoining walled garden and outdoor dining area. As they made their way to the new café, the air filled with the scents of baking bread and pastries. Walking up to the entrance, the scents of brewing coffee and fresh bread wafted from within, drawing them inside. "Oh, this is making my stomach rumble with all these good smells."

Anne nodded, "Me too. Let's hope it tastes as well as it smells."

They walked up to the blond hostess named Suzette, who greeted them with a "Bonjour. Welcome to the French Bistro. Two?"

"Yes, please." Anne replied.

She waited as the elegant young woman looked at the chart on her hostess stand. "Would you like to sit inside or outside?"

While the walk over had been nice, they were both wearing jackets. "What do you think, Kandi? It could be a bit chilly outside."

"No, madam. There is a large fireplace out there and we also have heaters situated around the edges. The walls keep the heat trapped in there and with the umbrellas down, the light also provides a warm sun trap. But if you prefer inside—"

"I'm game if you are." Kandi replied.

"Okay, if nothing else, we can keep our jackets on." Anne followed the woman, who was dressed in a blue shift with matching ballet flats. Scanning the interior as they made their way past booths and tables, they were led through doors that brought them out onto a sunny flagstone area.

"Ladies, enjoy your meal." Suzette beckoned them to the table as they were greeted by a server with a towel over his arm.

"Bonjour. I am Maitre d'hotel." He spoke French so quickly that the pair had difficulty understanding exactly what he had said. Anne was grateful when he switched over to English. "Would you prefer sparkling or plain?" He gestured to their water goblets.

Anne responded. "Sparkling, please."

"Sure, I guess." Kandi cast her gaze around the restaurant, noting the other diners.

After the server had poured their water, he handed them menus and then directed their attention to the board over on the wall of the building with specials of the day. It was written in French but still easy to understand.

After he left, Kandi whispered to Anne. "He's pretty hunky, huh?"

"I hadn't noticed."

Kandi made a face. "Then you have to be dead. That guy is drop dead gorgeous."

"Okay, maybe he's a bit handsome." She grinned.

Kandi glanced around. "I'm seeing dollar signs here. Pretty fancy for, like, breakfast."

"I don't think Polly would have recommended it if it was outrageous on pricing. Plus, it's nice to see a service like this for a change. Sometimes it feels like they're doing you a favor by waiting on you. Now, what are you going to have? My treat."

"Oh, in that case—" Kandi winked and opened her menu.

They perused the list of options, but both decided to go with Polly's suggestion of the Gruyere omelet. Kandi pulled out her phone. "I'm wondering who that was this morning."

"Me too. Anything on social media?"

Kandi shook her head. "Nope. Let me pull up the addresses." She opened her Maps app and glanced at the houses. Tapping her finger to her chin, she looked up to the right, thinking. "If I remember correctly, it was almost to the crest of the hill on Bells. We were turning onto Market Street, so that limits the houses to this group."

Kandi set the phone down on the table, and Anne leaned over to look at the various houses. So, if we count back from the top of the hill, it's most probably this house or this—"Oh, no. It couldn't be!"

"What is it?"

"If it's this house, I know the person. They were at Hope's mushroom class. Let me think. What was her name—um, Laura, ah, Lauren..." Kandi gasped. "Laurel!"

"Who's Laurel?"

"She was a participant at the mushroom class Hope held at her shop. I don't know what happened, but at some point, she and Hope got into an argument. Everyone heard them, even though Hope had asked her to step into the back. She'd come storming out and left the class after that."

The conversation ceased as a young woman appeared, holding their meals. As the server set down their plates, the sight of the omelet and rosemary potatoes artfully arranged on the plates looked delightful. When Kandi reached out to take hold of her silverware, it made a loud clattering sound as it fell to the ground.

"Kandi, what's wrong? You look like you've seen a ghost. Are you okay? You're pale."

"No. I mean, yes. I'm okay. I'm just thinking about their last words." She retrieved the cutlery as another server brought her a new set. After she'd departed, Kandi took a sip of her water.

"What did they say?"

"Laurel said that Hope was going to be sorry."

"And?"

"Hope said, 'I think you're the one who's going to be sorry.'"

Anne replied, "Well, that doesn't mean anything."

Kandi stared into Anne's face. "That wasn't all Hope said."

"So, what else?"

"For the rest of your short, sad life."

CHAPTER THREE

Anne waited as another one of the staff returned with coffee and a small pitcher of cream. Slowly stirring in the cream to her freshly made black coffee, she carefully took a sip of the warm drink. This gave her the opportunity to contemplate all of Kandi's words before responding. "I don't know. That certainly doesn't sound like the Hope I've come to know and appreciate."

In response, Kandi nodded her head in agreement. "I know. That was what made the situation so odd. To begin with, it was completely unexpected for them to fight. And then Hope shouted at her, like, with everyone watching."

"There has to be something we don't know about. Because Hope is not one to make a scene." Anne thought about the missed calls. What is going on with Hope?

"You're right, it's not something she usually does, it's not her typical behavior. This was completely out of the ordinary for her. I've never seen her act like that before."

Taking the freshly starched cloth napkin, Anne carefully unfolded it and placed it in her lap. "All of us are subject to having days that are hard, it is unavoidable, and there is no one who is exempt from this. Even Hope."

"I know, but this just seemed different somehow. Had the mycelium group not been present, Hope would have definitely asked everyone, not just Laurel, to leave. I could see she was really upset."

"This has me even more worried about her. Perhaps we could make a brief detour to her shop before heading back. Let's see if we can figure out what is going on."

Kandi gave a slight inclination of her head in agreement and then began to cut the omelet into pieces. As she slowly and carefully used her fork to pick up the bite, the gooey cheese easily separated itself from the rest of the food on her plate. Using her fork to cut the egg dish, she then cautiously brought it to her mouth to take a bite. "Oh woah. That is something else."

Anne took great care to ensure that she could spear a piece of asparagus with her fork before taking a bite of her omelet. "Oh wow. You are so right. My taste buds are in heaven with this amazing flavor! I can certainly see why this is Polly's favorite." She cut another bite and popped it into her mouth, enjoying the mix of flavors before spearing one of the rosemary potatoes. "I'm glad I picked these potatoes as my side. They're just as good. It's like a bit of crunch on the outside, but almost like mashed potatoes on the inside. So good." She used her fork to take another bite.

When the waiter came over to her table with a basket with a crisp, white towel on top, she was just about to have another bite of her meal. "We are sorry to have kept you waiting for your croissants, ladies. Are you finding the food to your liking?"

"Delicious." They mumbled behind their hands as they finished chewing.

"Wonderful. Please let me know if you require anything else." He bowed and moved off.

Kandi carefully wiped her mouth with the napkin before she began to speak. "Is there an unspoken rule that waiters should ask if they can get anything else while people still have food in their mouths?"

"Yes, I think it's in the codebook for waiter training." Anne took another drink of her coffee.

"Really?" Kandi asked.

Anne grinned before taking another bite of food.

"Oh, my gosh. I can't believe I fell for that. Now hand over one of those yummy looking croissants."

After taking extra care to place the basket in front of Kandi, Anne watched as Suzette stepped onto the patio. Anne couldn't help but be drawn to the three women she was leading, as their behavior was extraordinary, and they seemed to have an aura of confidence about them.

The vast number of new people in the town made it difficult to keep up with the locals and the increasing number of tourists. One woman, in particular, seemed to differ from the rest. The woman was wearing expensive clothing, shoes, and carried a designer handbag, which made it clear that she was wealthy and wanted others to be aware of it.

Kandi lowered her voice. "Oh, her again."

"Who?"

Kandi lowered her voice as she shared, "Her name's Miranda."

"Miranda? Why does that name sound familiar?"

"Because we walked by her new place coming over her. She's setting up an apothecary, just like Hope. Though most of her current herbal items are cosmetic versus for health. I don't know. I get a bad feeling about her for some reason."

Anne's eyes followed Suzette as she led the women to a table tucked away in the corner. All the other women held back until Miranda had decided on where to sit before they took their seats. From their manner of showing her deference, it was obvious that she was the leader of the group.

She returned her attention to Kandi. "Well,

it's not like we can't have more than one store of each kind in town. In fact, sometimes it helps business. That's why you often see two of the same type, like a drugstore for instance. You'll have two stores on opposite sides of the same street. Though I'm still not clear on how it's supposed to work to bring in more business."

Kandi stared longingly at the now empty basket where the bread had been. "I wonder if we can get more croissants?"

"You are hungry, aren't you?" Anne cut another piece of her omelet.

Kandi shrugged. "I guess so."

"Once he has taken their order, we can look at getting some more bread, or if you'd prefer, you have the option of getting a dessert."

"Oh, let me think about that."

The women's laughter carried over from their table as they chatted with the waiter., who had a strange look on his face. Maybe he didn't want to deal with people who thought they were your betters. Miranda barely looked at him before stating, "We'll have a lovely bottle of Prosecco and some orange juice, please."

"Excellent, mademoiselle."

"Mademoiselle, my foot." Anne huffed. "I think that waiter's just trying to garner a bigger tip."

"Now, now. Don't be 'meow.'" She put her hands up like claws.

That elicited a chuckle from Anne. "Funny. But I'm not being catty. She has to be my age."

"Maybe he did it because she's not wearing a ring."

"Possibly. I hadn't even noticed. But I think it's more that he's just expecting a bigger tip due to the blatant 'I'm wealthy' vibe."

Kandi huffed. "I may not be right. But one thing I'm right about is that she was also at the mushroom class, along with the ladies with her."

Anne bit into her flaky croissant. "Oh, this is heaven. No wonder you want to see about getting another one." She wiped the crumbs from her mouth before continuing, "It doesn't surprise me that people want to come to classes at Hope's. She always makes sure that the information is good before she'll open her doors to anyone."

"I suppose, like, I wish I knew what to think." She signaled to the waiter, who appeared with another basket of croissants. "I believe I heard you say you would like some more of these. Enjoy." He smiled before turning around and heading off to another table.

A bright rush of color filled Anne's face as she blushed. "Oh, crud. I hope that he didn't overhear my rant about how he was trying to impress those women."

"Well, it's too late to put that chicken back in the coop. You better, like, give him a good tip now." Kandi smiled as she broke another croissant in half over her plate.

"Let's quit talking about that and enjoy the rest of this lovely meal."

Kandi nodded. "I like that idea. Plus, I think it would be good to stop by Hope's and see how she's doing."

"Agree. Plus, I could use some more of her women's tea blend."

"Good. Don't want the cranky Anne to show

up." Kandi winked.

"Ha. Ha. One day, you'll have to deal with hormones like this."

"Yep, but not for many, many, um, many years."

Anne made an expression of exasperation and rolled her eyes. "Many, many, huh? Are you intending to walk home?"

Kandi giggled.

"What did you decide about dessert?"

"I think I'm good now that I've had this second croissant."

Anne motioned for the waiter to come over to their table, and he hastened there with a pleasant smile gracing his lips. It was undeniable that he was an attractive man.

"Yes, ladies. May I interest you in some dessert?"

"Maybe next time. For now, the bill, please."

"Certainly. May I?" After gaining permission to remove their plates, he picked them up before leaving to gather their bill. When he returned, he set two small plates in front of them with a petit four on it with the initials FB on it. He left and Anne pulled her card out and slotted it into the little plastic case.

Using the small fork from the dessert plate to pick up the cake bite, she popped it into her mouth. Immediately, the taste of sweet orange along with the buttercream filled her senses.

"That's amazing. It's like they are trying to hit every sense. The only thing missing is, like, sound."

The waiter returned once again. He left the case on the table with a blue and gold pen with the name French Bistro on it. "Thank you for dining with us today. Revenez s'il vous plaît." He bowed and left.

"What did he say?" Kandi asked, picking up her bag and putting it over her shoulder.

"I know the last part is please, so most likely something like come again, please. I guess that adding in of the French words adds to the ambience. Whoever owns this place has thought of everything." After signing for their meal and leaving a nice tip, Anne put her card away. Joining

Kandi, they made their way out of the restaurant that was now filled with a few guests waiting for tables.

"Looks like we picked the right time to come here. Oh shoot. I forgot my jacket. Back in a jiff." Anne made her way out to the patio, where her jacket still hung from the back of the chair. On her way out, she stole a glance at Miranda and her friends.

Was that why Hope had been on edge that day?

Maybe she didn't like the idea of a competitor against her shop. Or maybe something else had triggered Hope's outburst.

The question remained. What had caused Hope to say the things she'd said?

CHAPTER FOUR

As soon as she put on her jacket, she passed by a group of people who were on their way into the restaurant. If the quality of food being served and the long lines of customers were any indication, this place was definitely a successful establishment. She moved around a group of ladies chatting outside, their voices bubbling with the joy that comes from getting together with women friends. After finding Kandi standing out front, the two of them were on their way, walking down the street toward Anne's car.

Anne opened the doors, and she sighed with pleasure as she felt the warmth on her back. "That meal was so good. I definitely want to come back again and try other things on their menu. Plus, did you see the dessert case close to the front door? I had to hurry past it, or I would have asked for one of each!"

Kandi yawned. "Yes, they looked delicious."

Anne put on her signal and waited for a break in the traffic before pulling out onto the street. As they drove back toward the house they had noticed earlier, they were silent. At the corner, they both turned their heads to where everything had happened. All the emergency vehicles were gone. The street now appeared indistinguishable from all the other streets, just like it was any other day.

Anne made a right turn onto the street, leaving the house in their rear view. Glancing over at Kandi, she noted that the young woman, usually so chatty, had her eyes closed. She wondered if Kandi hadn't slept well or possibly needed some vitamins. Though all that bread could have caused her blood sugar to make her sleepy.

Focusing back on the drive, she thought about the earlier event. What terrible event had occurred that lead to someone's death? The person in question seemed to be quite young if Kandi's guess was correct. In a relatively short time, they had navigated their way to Hope's

Herbal Shoppe.

"We're here, sleepyhead."

Kandi blinked for a minute before wiping her face with her hands. She yawned loudly. "Must not have gotten enough sleep." She followed Anne out of the vehicle.

As they walked into the store, they heard the peaceful and melodic sound of the chimes ringing in the air. Along the wall of the store, a variety of glass jars were visible and seemed to glisten in the light, each of them holding various herbs that could be used for teas, tisanes, and other remedies that could be purchased in large quantities. In other shelves, brown bottles held various tinctures to aid mind or body. Among the large wooden tables, a few people browsed through the selection of soaps crafted from goat's milk and those with lavender petals.

A clerk of Hope's was busy helping a customer and Hope herself was nowhere to be found. They meandered throughout the room, yet Hope didn't make her way to the front of the space. While disappointed that Hope wasn't available, it was possible that she was occupied with one of her patients in the back where she had her office. If so, they probably wouldn't have time to speak with her.

After the current shopper had been served, Anne went forward to the counter and took her place in the line. After the woman had departed, Anne directed a greeting towards the young woman who'd waited on the customer, saying, "Hello Autumn. I didn't know that you were back at this job again."

"I feel like I would benefit from having some interactions with people of my age group, if you get what I'm saying."

Even though Anne had never been a parent, she could imagine what it would be like to have twins and the amount of effort it would take to look after them. "I do. And good to see you here. Is Hope around?"

She is occupied with some work in the back and has asked not to be disturbed. Autumn shifted her body and leaned in closer to Anne, lowering her voice confidentially. "I'm uncertain if I should share this information, but since you're her friend, I feel that you should know. Recently she has not been like her usual self, it's as if she has changed. I can't put my finger on it. It's just a feeling."

Anne gave a slight movement of her head in agreement. "Got it. Kandi said something similar to me. I've been attempting to get in touch with her for the last few days, but I haven't been successful thus far."

As they conversed, a female figure emerged at the back door, grasping a bag in her hand. Hope stood behind her. "I look forward to seeing you again in a week's time." When she spotted Anne, instead of approaching her, she made a detour back towards her office.

"Hope, wait up!" Rushing over to reach her, Anne made her way to where Hope stood by the office door. "Hi. Whew. You've been hard to get hold of for the last few days. Got a minute?"

Hope's face bore a strange look Anne wasn't expecting. Hope hesitated, then responded, "I'm sorry, but I have quite a lot of things to take care of and I'm not free to talk at the moment. "

Anne was taken aback by Hope's sudden and unexpected behavior. Kandi was right. This wasn't the Hope that always took time for others. "I don't want to be a nuisance if you currently have other engagements. I'm just curious to know if it would be possible for you to make an additional batch of that special women's blend tea. I'm just about out and I don't see it out in the jars on the shelf."

In an angry tone, Hope blurted out, "Oh, sure. It's not like I have anything else on my schedule. Allow me to take care of that immediately."

Anne's forehead creased in concentration as her eyebrows knotted together, and her mouth formed a frown. Hope's response was unlike anything Anne had ever seen of her before. "I didn't mean that I wanted it done right away. Just asking when you might have some more available."

The sound of Hope's phone ringing interrupted their exchange. She answered it, holding up a finger to Anne. "Hello. Yes. What?

I'll be over soon." Exhaling a weary sigh, she tenderly massaged her eyes with her hands.

"Hope, I—"

Hope blurted out in frustration. "Anne, can't you see I'm busy? And now this. I can't spend my days like you do just running after people. I have a business to run. No, make that businesses."

Anne stepped back, not wanting to draw more attention to their conversation. "I don't know what to say."

"That's right, you don't. Because you don't know. You need to understand that not everything revolves around you, Anne. Now I have to work." With determined strides, Hope marched towards her office and shut the door behind her, leaving Anne standing there, confused, and in turmoil.

What could possibly be the reason Hope was acting so oddly? And more importantly, what had she done to upset Hope?

Kandi cautiously peered around the corner. "Is everything okay?"

Anne struggled to respond. No, it certainly was not. But there was nothing she could do about it now. For some unknown reason, Hope was avoiding her, and she had to get to the heart of the matter to find out why.

~~

Arriving back at the house, Anne waved at the new neighbors across the street from her. The owner who had been renting out the home to a group of people had finally decided to sell the house. A couple with young children had moved into the house, and the cul-de-sac that had once been quiet now rang with children's laughter as they rode their bikes or played in the yard.

Anne's elderly neighbors, usually cranky about noise, had taken to the children like wildfire, becoming surrogate grandparents. Often she'd see the kids on the porch, with the gentlemen reading stories to them and the woman sneaking them cookies before dinner. The young mother must have appreciated the couple's help, as she had her hands full with another new baby, along with getting everything settled in the house. Though she'd often be heard yelling out as the kids scampered over next door, "No cookies today, gran." Thus, most days, the older woman had sent home a plate full of cake or some other food item for the family.

Anne made it into the house with her bag from Polly's only to have Mouser greet her at the kitchen door, wrapping his slinky body around her legs.

"Let me get into the house first before you beg, okay?" She picked him up, stroking his black head for a moment as she listened to his purrs of contentment. Pulling a round tray with slots in it from the bag, she sprinkled a bit of catnip over the top and placed the ball in the slot. Setting it over in the room's corner, Mouser went right to it, first batting at the ball with his paw and then laying his entire body on top of the new toy. Anne laughed at his antics. "I hope I'm not your dealer now. But enjoy it."

She hung up her jacket and then used the back stairs to make her way up to the second floor. Carson had helped her fulfill a dream as the door to the landing had been recovered in green baize as it had been originally when the house was first built, and English settlers had brought their servants over with them. What a different time that was. She opened the door and stepped out onto the landing to hear the soft tones of classical music playing in the air. It was still weird to have Carson here in the house with her, but in a good way.

After some consideration, they'd decided to stay in Anne's house, renting out his house for tourists. His house in the woods was a lovely escape from the day to day and soon a group of writers were preparing to take over the house for a writer's retreat. Now that Carson had finally decided to pursue his dream of becoming a crime fiction author, it made sense to allow writers to use it for mastermind weekends and retreats.

When Anne stepped into the room, Carson immediately raised his gaze from his computer. "Hey there, you!" He held out his hand to her.

"Hey, back at ya." With a gentle embrace, he lifted her up and planted a kiss on her forehead as she took a seat in his lap.

"How's the writing process coming along?"

"It looks like it should be a straightforward task, but it is, in fact, more challenging than it appears. Every day you have to come to the computer and words have to come out of your fingertips like some magic."

"Don't forget you're talking to someone that's written books. But I would have to think creating worlds out of thin air is more difficult than talking about suburban homesteading or more how-to style books." She pointed at the words on the screen. "You've already made great progress. Can I read some of it now?"

With a slight shake of his head, he replied, "Nope. Not yet. Let me get the first draft completed and a pass-through edit and then I'll hand it over to you for your insights. How was breakfast?"

"Wonderful. We'll have to go there for dinner sometime. The food was delicious."

He swiveled his chair away from the desk. "What's bothering you?"

She shook her head, chuckling. "How is it you know me so well?"

"I can see it in your face. Something's on your mind. What is it?"

"It's Hope. She's been avoiding me and today she was snippy with me."

"Snippy?"

"Right? You would never think of her that way. But yes, snippy. I've never known her to act the way she did. It actually shocked me."

"Hmm, maybe you did or said something that upset her. And you know how she is, Hope's never been one to confront anyone about anything."

"I've thought of that. But I've been racking my brain trying to figure it out. I don't have a clue what the issue might be."

"Well, how about I take your mind off of it for now?"

"What do you have in mind?"

He smiled.

CHAPTER FIVE

With only a few dishes left to be washed in the sink, Anne heard a knock coming from the back door. Stewart lagged slightly behind Kandi as she proceeded into the room.

"Hi guys."

Glancing around the room, Stewart asked, "Is Carson here?"

"Unfortunately, no. He is required to be on duty a few times and this is one night he's working."

Although Carson had been hoping to retire from his position as Sheriff, Deputy Ruiz had asked him to remain in the role of sheriff for one more term. This way, it would be an easier transition for Deputy Ruiz from the undersheriff to the sheriff. Carson had agreed as long as it became a part-time job once they could find more staff, intending to quit afterwards so he and Anne could experience more traveling while they were still young and able.

"Okay, well, I'll probably head on home then. Call me and I'll come walk you home when you're ready."

As Kandi watched him leave, she signaled her understanding with a slight nod.

Anne's face slightly contorted as her eyebrows rose, arching her forehead. "That seems to be a bit excessive, don't you think? It's not that far, you're only two doors away from me. What's caused this sudden and increased attention and focus?"

"He's only wanting, like, to take care of me. That's all." Kandi blushed.

Anne fixed her gaze on Kandi, who was clearly trying to suppress the smile that threatened to appear on her face. In a moment of realization, Anne's mouth dropped open as the pieces of the puzzle all fit together. "You little minx. You're pregnant, aren't you?"

Kandi's face suddenly lit up with a huge grin. "I told Stewart I would stay silent until I was completely sure, but I am reasonably sure. The results of the tests I've taken have been quite varied and inconsistent. But deep down in my heart, I know it's true." She sighed. "I hope he won't be like this the entire time, fussing over me."

Anne gathered Kandi up in an embrace, tears of joy streaming down her face. "Oh, my gosh. I'm so happy for you and Stewart. And let him fuss. It's just showing how much he loves you."

Kandi gently wiped away the tears that had fallen from her eyes as the two of them separated. "I'm still trying to wrap my mind around it. Me. A mom. I worry if I can, like, do it."

"Of course, you can. You'll be a wonderful mother." Anne hugged Kandi again. "I'm so happy for you guys. Now, sit down. What do you need? Are you feeling okay?"

"Oh, no. I hope you're not going to be like Stewart! He's been hovering around me for the last week."

"Sorry. I, oh my gosh. A baby. How exciting for you both."

"You know what this makes you, right? You'll be a grandma."

"Ack! Wait, is that what all the 'you're old' was

about? I can't even imagine that."

"Well, you better, because the months will fly by. And you'll want to figure out what you want to be called."

"I think the child usually chooses your name for you. But we'll see." Anne clapped her hands together. "This calls for a celebration. Hot Fudge or Banana Split?"

"I know this is going to sound a little strange, but do you have any green olives? It's been on my mind all day, and I'm really craving those."

Anne made her way to the pantry, looking through the cans and jars to determine if there were any green olives. She responded, "In actuality, green olives have an element that can help to ease any stomach upset you may be experiencing. Have you been experiencing any signs of sickness early in the morning?"

Kandi rapped her knuckles on the table. "No, thank goodness. But maybe that's why I've been wanting olives all the time."

Extracting a jar from the cabinet, Anne held it in her hands. "Success! I found some. These have pimentos in them. Hope that's okay."

Kandi gave a slight shrug of her shoulders. "I guess we'll see." Taking a seat at the table, she accepted a small plate and two-tined fork from Anne before she opened the jar. She picked out a few of the olives and placed them on the plate before popping one in her mouth. She sighed with pleasure. "Oh, yes. Perfect."

Anne went back over to the pantry and found some crackers. She put them on the table. "Anything else you might like?"

"Pickles?" Kandi popped another olive in her mouth.

Anne pulled a jar of bread and butter pickles from the fridge, adding them to the growing collection of items on the table. "Anything else?"

"I'm good for now. Except maybe some butter for the crackers."

After Anne had placed the butter and a knife on the table, she took a seat opposite Kandi. "Were you just coming over to visit? Or was something else on your mind?"

Kandi sat up in her chair, her face bearing a

look of anticipation. "I wanted to tell you I found out that it was Laurel that we saw them taking out of her house this morning."

"Were you able to find out what happened?"

"They're still looking into it, but they think she may have eaten some toxic mushrooms." She slathered a cracker with butter before popping it in her mouth.

"That's horrible. I wonder why they think that?" Anne rose and pulled some iced tea from the fridge. "Is this okay, since it has caffeine in it?"

"I'll be okay." Kandi took a sip of the drink before popping another olive into her mouth. "I believe they found some in her garbage. I'm sure they'll be doing some testing on it. Plus, I heard from the dispatcher that she'd called for help."

Anne was still amazed that Kandi could get so much insider information, but that's what came from growing up in Carolan Springs and knowing everyone. "That's horrible if it's true. Did she go out and collect some mushrooms on her own without verifying if they were edible?"

"No idea. Of course, they won't know what

really happened until the tests come back."

Anne placed her hands in front of her and clasped them together on the table. Could you tell me how you stumbled upon this information? I mean, I know you have a boatload of sources, but just curious."

Kandi licked the cracker crumbs from her lips. "Sam relayed this news to me."

"Sam?" Anne asked. "I thought he'd moved to DC permanently, and that he was pursuing a relationship with that agent."

"I guess it just wasn't meant to be, and it didn't turn out the way he thought it would. He didn't say much about that, but he decided to move back here. He missed Colorado and the mountains. Plus, he's a big skier in the winter."

Anne said, "I didn't know he was back in town."

"Well, why would you?" Kandi took another drink of iced tea.

That was indeed true. Even though Anne and Sam had had a short-lived relationship when she had moved to Carolan Springs, she had only ever had feelings for one man.

"No matter. Anyway, back to Laurel. It sounds like a tragic accident. Sad, but people think they have more knowledge than they do and go off doing something foolish like this. And sadly, it got her killed. So, most likely, no mystery there."

"Maybe. I don't know. Although I didn't know her that well, it didn't seem likely that she would venture off into the woods and search for mushrooms without someone in the know with her."

Anne responded with a nod of her head. "True. But it's feasible that she might have taken up this new hobby and thought she knew which were edible. People do sometimes think that they know more than they really do. Just curious though. Why do they think it was mushrooms that killed her?"

Kandi shrugged. "I don't know. But there must have been something that tipped them off. Though I'm sure they'll find out more once they get the tests back."

Anne placed her back against the chair, her body taking in the support as she allowed herself to rest against it. "Despite the circumstances, it's still quite a sad situation. Did she have any close family members living here?"

"As far as I am aware, no. I think her parents are elderly and living in Florida. Why?"

"It occurred to me it'll be necessary for someone to pack up her belongings. If she doesn't have family close by. Plus, not sure if they'll allow her friends to do it." Anne carefully popped an olive into her mouth, taking her time to savor its flavor as she chewed it.

Kandi snorted, "You want to snoop in her house!"

"Well, aren't you curious? I mean, she goes to a mushroom class at Hope's and the next thing you know, she's dead and it's most likely attributed to poison mushrooms. You don't think she meant to eat them? You know, on purpose?"

"No. I can't see that. She was looking forward to a trip she wanted to take. I overheard her telling the people in the class that she's been saving up and selling items online to get the money together. She wouldn't say it, but I think she was planning a trip with someone she'd met. No, unless something changed fairly recently, I never saw or heard her say anything that would make me think that."

Would it be possible for you to give Sam a call and find out if he knows any details regarding her parents? If they are older, we would be helping them immensely by taking care of this for them."

"Along with being nosy?"

"Okay, yes. I have a big curious. Plus, maybe this could help with a plot for Carson's next book." She winked.

"Fine. I'll call Sam tomorrow morning. Now, where's that ice cream and hot fudge?"

CHAPTER SIX

The next morning, Anne buzzed with excitement. Even though Carson had his work and new endeavor with writing, she'd not been enthused to start anything new of her own. People knew that it was usually too early to plant before Mother's Day, so they waited a bit longer before calling for help with their gardens. Any plants that are not hardy could be damaged or even destroyed if a snowstorm strikes unexpectedly.

She had to face the fact that her nosiness was just as Kandi had said. She was driven by her curiosity to solve any kind of mystery and enjoyed the challenge of trying to figure things out. She enjoyed taking the individual parts and assembling them to produce an outcome that was clear. Even if it was just to verify what everyone already knew to be accurate. She hadn't felt this excited in a while to investigate another mystery, and the prospect of it made her giddy. She wasn't certain what it said about her as an individual.

Probably no different from those people who binged on true crime shows.

However, she knew that it made her feel valued when she could discover something that had been overlooked. If she could bring out the truth or ensure that nothing was missed, it had to be helpful. Even if Carson and the police hadn't seen it as helping, but more like meddling. Thankfully, she'd never gotten into so much that she'd been arrested for it.

After much thought, she decided to try speaking with Hope again. Perhaps they could visit the Herbal Shoppe and treat Hope to a lunch date. She texted Kandi, who still hadn't heard back from Sam yet. After informing Kandi that she was going to the grocery store, and inquiring if she wanted any olives, she grabbed the list of items she had compiled earlier and slid it into her bag. She quickly grabbed the shopping bags that were tucked away by the back door and went out to her SUV.

After making her way into town, she was relieved to find that the main traffic had already passed, allowing her to get to Hope's in a timely manner. When she arrived, she was dismayed to observe that the store had a Closed sign on the door. She had completely forgotten that the store would not open until later in the day on Thursdays. She drove around to the back of Hope's flat and eventually arrived at the entrance door. Autumn must have also just arrived as she bent down, chaining her bike to a post close to the back door.

Taking a deep breath, Anne opened the car door and stepped out of her vehicle. "That's an impressive bike you have there."

Autumn rose from the ground, stretching her back. "It's from the Netherlands. It's perfect for hauling things, and I am looking forward to attaching the carrier to the back of it so I can take my twins out for rides soon."

"I must say, I'm deeply impressed. With the demands of looking after young children, I'm not sure I would have the energy to do that much exercise."

"Biking helps calm my mind and since we

don't live far, I can take the paved trailways over here and skip out on the traffic issues."

"I certainly understand that. We had to deal with that traffic yesterday. Oh, that reminds me. Were you here for the presentation and the mushroom class?"

"Yes, why?" Autumn bent over and touched the ground with her flat hands.

Anne gazed in awe at the flexibility of the young woman. It was a good reminder that she needed to do more stretching. She wasn't even sure she could touch her toes anymore. "Yesterday, when we were driving over here, we saw a person being removed from their home. Wait, let me rephrase that. They had passed away, and they were taking away the body. It was Laurel. Sorry, I don't know her last name. Did you know her?"

"No, can't say I know her, but I recall a Laurel being at the meeting." Autumn grabbed her ankle and effortlessly pulled her leg up into the dancer's pose. "If I remember correctly, I think she came in late." She switched legs. "In fact, I don't think she paid for the class. She just showed up and then mingled with everyone else."

"Is that why she and Hope had words?"

"Could have been." She reached her arm over her back, clasping her hands behind her. "I don't think I've ever heard Hope raise her voice. But she, let's see, she said something like, 'why would you do such a thing' but Laurel just told her to mind her own business. That's when Hope really lost her cool. But I didn't hear what they said next as I was passing out some drinks with chaga mushroom to the guests. All I remember was Laurel stomping out of the back and slumping into one of the chairs. I know Hope wanted her to leave, but she was a guest of the speaker, so couldn't do anything about it."

Anne thought back. So Laurel hadn't left like Kandi thought. "Who all attended the talk?"

Autumn switched her arms to stretch the other side of her body. "Oh, let me think. Of course, the speaker, Marcia Landers. Then she had a few guests with her, so Laurel and two other ladies and a few gentlemen. There were a few couples attending, not sure of their names—and then Miranda, and two women who came with her. Hope wasn't happy about Miranda being there."

"Because of her opening her shop?"

"Maybe. But it seemed like something else. Although I have my suspicions, I can't be certain, as Hope's never directly stated her opinion. Hope has so much to handle and having to cope with competition is just one more thing she has to deal with." Autumn sauntered over to the back entrance, producing the key and turning it in the lock to open the door. "Come on in. Are you here to pick up a package or grab some herbs?"

"No. I stopped by to talk with Hope."

"Oh, sorry. I probably could have saved you some time. She's not here."

"No worries. When will she be back?"

"Not sure. She said she'd be leaving for a few days and to see if I could get one of the part-time staff to help at the store and, if not, to just close up the shop."

"That's strange. She didn't say anything else?"

"Nope." Autumn activated the lights in the back kitchen area with a quick flick of her finger. An array of bottles, ranging in various colors, sizes, and shapes, were along one extended bench, all holding herbal remedies that would eventually be brewed into tinctures once the liquid had been infused with the herbs. In the far corner of the room, a box was open, with a few baskets peeking out of the top.

"Oh, those are wonderful baskets." Anne confidently strode over and picked the item up, taking a moment to appreciate its details.

"Yes, that was part of the gift from the presentation. Going out foraging for food or mushrooms and holding supplies is made easier with these baskets. Each person who was present received one. Well, all the individuals who'd gone through the Shoppe in order to purchase something. For anyone who wanted to buy one then, they had the option to purchase one that day or they could place an order for one. We had not expected such an overwhelming demand and ran out of stock that day."

Anne set the basket down. "I doubt I'll do any foraging, but these baskets would make great gifts for my garden design clients. I'll see if I can find out from Hope where she got them."

"Sounds good. Now I better get started before I have to open. Anything else?"

"No. Thanks for the info. Have a great day."

"You too." Autumn waved farewell as she moved in the direction of the Shoppe's main entrance.

Taking her time to close the door, Anne started to move towards her vehicle. After entering her car, she rummaged through her purse to find her phone, then called Hope. The phone went directly to voice mail.

Anne's face clouded over with a deep frown. If she can't connect with her through the phone, then she should try texting her instead. She punched in her message.

> Hope. Sorry to miss you. Wasn't aware you were planning a trip out of town. Let's chat soon.

After a moment of reflection, she punched in some more words.

If I've done something, please let
me know. Love, Anne.

Anne waited, but there was no reply.

Despite her best efforts, she had done all she could do. She had to finish her errands before she could find out what Kandi had discovered. The sound of her SUV filled the alleyway as she started it up and drove away. A glint caught her attention.

A broken bottle lying on the ground shone in the bright sunlight of the morning. There was something about it that seemed familiar. She brought her vehicle to a stop and got out of her car by opening the door. It was definitely a bottle from the Herbal Shoppe, there was no doubt about it. Anne moved closer to the broken bottle. Glancing up at the barrier behind the area, she saw a stain on the concrete wall. Had the bottle been hurled out of a window? What could have caused someone doing something like that? It was highly unlikely that Hope would have taken the time to create something, only to then immediately destroy it. None of it made any sense whatsoever.

Convinced that recording this was necessary, she retrieved her phone. Pulling up the camera function, she captured an image of the stain on the wall and the shattered bottle that lay on the ground. Moving to the backseat of her car, she retrieved the paper towels she kept stored there and then picked up the bottle, securely storing it in a box on the backseat floorboard. It was probably nothing but better to find that out than to let a clue be lost forever.

CHAPTER SEVEN

Anne made it home after spending way too much on a few groceries. Now that she was buying for her and Carson, she had to get back to regular grocery shopping and she was shocked at the costs of things. Often she'd grabbed something simple or had a smoothie but with Carson around he wanted "real food" as he called it. They'd agreed to split the chores so that he'd shop and cook one week, and she would do the next week. So far, the arrangement seems to have worked well. On the weekends, they'd cook and clean up together, which was also nice and made the effort not seem so much of a chore.

She parked by the back door and clicked open the doors so she could pull the groceries out from the side closest to the back door.

"Need help?" It was Kandi.

"Sure. That would be great. If you could take this bag and this container of soap, that would be helpful." Anne handed the items to Kandi, securing one bag on her arm before grabbing two more. She made it inside to the kitchen, where Kandi was setting the bags down on the kitchen table. "I'll go grab some more."

Anne replied, "How about you make us a cup of tea and I'll get the rest? Should only be one or two more trips."

"Okay, can do." Kandi moved to the sink and ran water into the kettle, putting it on to boil as Anne moved outside to retrieve the rest of the bags. She'd set the last bag on the floor when the kettle sounded that the water was ready.

"Let's grab our tea and go sit out on the back porch. That way Mouser can come outside and watch the birds by the feeder."

"Okay." Kandi made her tea with her usual heaping doses of cream and sugar while Anne drank her tea with no added items.

"Anything in there that needs to go in the fridge or freezer right now?" Kandi sipped her warm drink.

Anne pulled her feet up on the bench cushion beside her. "They can wait for a bit. I have the cold stuff with some ice packs and bags, so they'll be fine while we chat. What did you find out?"

"I called Sam, and he got me in touch with the landlord. Of course, they want the stuff moved out as soon as possible, so they can go in and get everything ready for the next tenant."

"Wow. That's compassionate. Not." Anne blew on her tea and sipped from the cup.

"It may not be great, but technically they didn't know her and what's the right amount of time to allot before they remove her items so they can rent the space?"

"Yes, I guess you're right. I don't know. It just seems so sad, I guess. All the stuff that we may treasure, others are ready to discard in an instant when we're gone. It's like removing their existence."

"That sounds more like something I'd say than you. What's, like, brought that on?"

"I don't know. It's just a good reminder to spend your time and effort on people instead of things." Anne smiled, but it didn't reach her eyes. "I must be a bit moody today. Let's get back on topic."

"Does this have anything to do with you being worried about Hope?"

Anne nodded. "She took off for a few days and didn't say anything. Did she call you?"

Kandi shook her head to the negative. "I'm sure she just wanted to get away for a bit."

"I don't know—"

"Well, not much we can do about it." Kandi continued, "Anyway, I told him that if the parents were okay with us packing everything up, we'd be happy to do it for them. No charge."

"What did you say was our reasoning for doing it?"

"I said that we knew her and didn't think she knew anyone else here that could help."

Anne chuckled. "Seriously? I think you could sell ice to people in Antarctica. When do we get access and what do they want us to do with her stuff? I don't mind helping, but I don't want to be stuck with a huge shipping fee."

Kandi responded by nodding her head in agreement as Mouser appeared on the back, entering through the open kitchen door. He rubbed his body against Kandi's legs, before bounding up to the bench where Anne sat, and then eventually perched on the ledge that Carson had made for him. He could watch the birds without them being disturbed by his presence because of his vantage point. He lay on the ledge and patiently waited for the birds to find their way to the feeder, though their arrival was unlikely since the day had grown late.

"They told the landlord if he could use her deposit to send personal items of hers and donate all the household goods and furniture to a local charity." Kandi teared up. "Those poor parents. I can't imagine what they're going through right now. Especially as they're so far away and unable to physically do anything."

"Don't make me cry, too. I'm already pretty emotional."

Kandi sniffed. "Why? Let me guess. Back to the Hope conversation?"

"I can't help it. I tried calling Hope and no answer and then I texted her and still no answer.

I don't know what I've done for her to be so upset with me. I've been racking my brain." Anne sat the cup down on the bench arm.

"What makes you think it has anything to do with you? It could be something else entirely, though I have to admit I can't figure out what's going on with Hope either."

Anne recrossed her legs. "Not much I can do about it for now, which is why this is helping me keep my mind occupied for a bit. I guess we should, or I should, let it go for now. I'm sure when Hope's ready to talk, she'll let us know. Anyway, just thinking out loud here, but I wonder if it would help Laurel's parents if we took a video of her place and maybe some things that showed that she was happy. What do you think?"

"I think that's a great idea. I can grab my camera and we can take a video of the place. This is when we could use Spencer's expertise. How's he doing, by the way?"

"Doing well. I can't believe he'll be graduating from college soon. Life is moving way too fast anymore."

Kandi yawned as she stood. "Let me help you put the groceries away and then I need to go home and take a nap."

Anne grinned. "Yep, definitely pregnant. You're like the energizer bunny so for you to need a nap is totally out of character."

"I go to the doctor this afternoon, so will know for sure then. Do you want to tackle this tomorrow or the next day?"

"Hmmm. Could Stewart help with the bigger pieces of furniture?"

Kandi nodded. "I'll see what his schedule's like for the next few days and recruit him to come help on that part. We should be able to get the little stuff done. I think it might be good to go over first thing tomorrow just to see how many boxes and things we'll need."

"Good idea. Now let's get this done so I can send you home to nap before your appointment."

As they entered the kitchen, a ding let Anne knew she had a text message. She picked up her phone.

"It's from Hope."

Kandi pulled cans from out of a bag. "What does it say?"

"Can't talk now."

"And?"

"And nothing. That's the entire text."

Kandi put her hands on her hips, looking as tough as a petite woman could look. "Okay, we've got to get to the bottom of this. Something's going on with Hope and we have to find out what it is."

~~

The following morning, Kandi picked Anne up in her truck. They would go over to pick up the keys from the landlord, and then get an idea of how many boxes and other items that were needed to pack everything up. Having the truck with them meant they could take some of the smaller furniture away if needed. They pulled up in the driveway, and Kandi turned off the truck. As the engine cooled, no one made a move.

Kandi glanced at the house before turning to Anne. "Am I, like, the only one, or do you feel a bit strange about doing this? It feels different now."

"Honestly? Yes. It's easy to talk about doing

something like this, but different when you face it. If you don't want to do this, we can hire someone. Since I got us into this mess, I'll pay for it."

Kandi shook her head, the messy bun bouncing up and down. "No. We've committed to it, and I don't enjoy going back on my word. Plus, she was one person, and it's a small home—only two bedrooms, so it shouldn't take that long. Let's do this." Kandi opened the door and stepped out onto the retractable truck step before planting her feet on the ground. Taking a deep breath, Anne watched as Kandi pulled out a small box with some odds and ends that she thought they might need.

On the other side of the vehicle, Anne pulled a tote bag that contained trash bags, a notepad and pen, some masking tape, and a few markers. They could at least pull the food from the fridge while they were here. She prayed the young woman wasn't messy, as who knew what would greet them if she was? Kandi strode over to the front door and stuck the key in the lock they'd retrieved from the landlord on the way over. The door opened easily, and Anne followed her into the front room.

Dust motes danced in the air, but Anne was grateful that the place looked neat and orderly. Just off the combination of living and dining areas, a bookcase held a collection of romance novels. A small kitchen lay farther at the back. To the right, a doorway revealed a hall. Most likely where the two bedrooms and bathroom were located. Kandi stepped over to the first door. Anne stopped her. "Let me go first. This was most likely her bedroom and we're not sure how the medical team left it."

"Good point. Not sure me and baby could handle something too hard this early in the morning." Kandi had phoned yesterday with the news that yes, she was pregnant. After okaying it with Stewart, Carson and Anne took them out for a celebratory dinner.

Anne peeked her head into the door that contained a double bed, one nightstand, a dresser with a large monitor on it, and a folding chair. Other than the sheets being messy from sleep, the room was neat too. "All clear. You want to check the bathroom, or should I do that first?"

"It's, fine. I'm going to check out the other bedroom first." As Kandi made her way toward the closed back door, Anne spied a journal on the bedside table. Scanning the last entry, she pondered the words written.

I don't know why I do it. I need to stop. I miss my family. I don't want to be a burden.

"Kandi, I've found her journal. She says she wants to stop something. Not sure what she means."

"I think I've found what she meant."

Anne flipped the pages back to the front when she felt movement against her bare legs.

She screamed.

Kandi jogged back down the hall to her. "What's the matter?"

"I felt something. I think she may have a rat in here. Oh, my gosh. That creeped me out." She fled from the room. In the living room, she took a breath and laughed. "Oh, good gravy. It was probably the mattress coverlet brushing up against my leg. Geez, I'm jumpy today."

"It's okay. I'm a bit jumpy too, but I want you to come and look at what I've found in the back room. Anne followed Kandi to the back room that comprised a set-up of various fold-up tables, with packing tape and other items. In the open closet, shelving held boxes of various sizes with post-it's on the front, stating the contents.

Anne swiveled back to look at the room before her mouth dropped open. "Is this what I think it is?"

Kandi nodded. "Yep, I think we've just found our porch pirate."

Anne joined Kandi, and they stared at a clipboard with items, addresses, and shipping information. As they bent over it, Kandi let out a cry.

"What is it?"

"Well, unless the mattress cover moved out of that room, something just went up against my legs, too."

Anne turned as a streak of color shot through the door of the room. "Wait a minute." She walked back into the front bedroom. Getting down on her knees, she peeked under the bed.

Two green eyes peered back at her.

"Hello, kitty."

CHAPTER EIGHT

Kandi came over and dropped to her knees alongside Anne by the bed.

"We're sorry we, like, screamed. You scared us." Kandi spoke soothingly, but the cat didn't move.

Anne dropped the cover back over it, thinking about how they could coax the feline to move from its spot in the corner. She peeked back under the bed, but the cat hadn't moved. It remained hunched down, and most likely would shoot out from under the bed if they moved it. She certainly didn't want to grab it and end up with scratches all over her. She dropped the bedspread again and crossed her legs as she sat back on the floor. "Well, I'm glad that it's not a rat. I don't know if we'll be able to coax it out. We should probably just call the landlord."

Kandi shook her head vehemently. "No. We can't do that. If I'm right, and I'm pretty sure I am, I bet that Laurel wasn't supposed to have any animals. Did you notice any bowls in the kitchen when we came in? And no toys or a scratching post. I'm betting that she didn't want her landlord to know she had a cat. I have a friend who lives in a duplex in the city, and they charge an extra fifty bucks a month to have an animal. And that's on top of the pet deposit."

"That's crazy. But I guess they do it to hinder people from having pets that could cause damage to the property." Anne drew herself up to her knees. "Poor thing. It's probably wondering what's going on. You're right. I didn't notice any bowls. We should look for those. We also need to see if there is any food or water for it. I didn't see anything. Did you?"

Kandi shook her head. "No, but like I said, she may have kept it hidden in case the landlord stopped by. Let's look."

"We can do that, but first, let's see if she has anything in the cabinets that we can feed it. Poor thing's probably hungry." Anne stood up and stretched her back before they made their way to the kitchen. She opened the fridge and spied a container marked 'tuna'. She opened it up, and it looked less like tuna and more like something else. She pulled the container from the fridge and opened it, giving it a good sniff. Ah, definitely a fishy smell. Laurel probably used that name on the container instead of cat food. Anne had to give it to her, it seemed that Laurel was extremely careful. It appeared that the food was still good. Pulling out a small plastic bowl from an upper cabinet, she scooped some of the food into it.

She set the bowl down on the floor and went back to the fridge, where she found milk that was still good. Using a saucer, she poured some into it. "Kandi, move out of the bedroom so it may come out for the food."

Kandi joined Anne in the kitchen, and they waited. Finally, she called, "Here kitty, kitty."

In a few minutes, the calico cat appeared. She gazed at them but didn't start eating. "Maybe we need to do something, so she doesn't feel all this attention. We're a bit like the waiters at a restaurant hovering too much."

"Good idea." Kandi reached over and opened

a cabinet. There were only a few dishes, some bowls, and glasses. "Well, this shouldn't be too bad. I think we can easily get this put into a few boxes. Speaking of, like, boxes, what should we do with the stuff in the back room?"

"Good question. Even though what she did was wrong, I don't want everyone talking about her until we find out more. Let's leave that room until the end and decide how to handle it. One idea might be to figure out if it could go back to its rightful owner and take it to the police. Though doesn't it seem funny that they didn't already do something about it?"

Kandi rocked her head side to side, her feather earrings catching the attention of the cat on the floor.

"'I'd be careful doing that or you may find a cat attached to your ear." Anne glanced over to see the cat crouched over the food, eating. Well, that was one good thing. She gazed down at the feline and spoke to Kandi. "First things first, what should we do with the cat? I guess we can call the rescue to come get it."

"Rescue? That poor thing has already been through a traumatic experience, doesn't know why its person just up and left and now you want to give it to a rescue? Why don't you take it?" Kandi's eyes glistened with tears.

Anne held her hands outstretched in front of her, making a sign for Kandi to stop. "Oh, no you don't! You're not going to guilt me into taking that cat with your hormonal waterworks."

"You said yourself that Mouser's hasn't seemed himself lately either. This would give him a playmate." Kandi wiped away the tears with the back of her hand.

Anne crossed her arms over her chest. "No. End of. I'm not having another cat. I don't need another cat. It isn't happening. You take it."

"I'm going to be having a baby. I don't need any more animals right now. Plus, Stewart wants to get a puppy at some point."

"Well, it's fine for now. Let's focus on what we came here to do." A meow stopped her.

Meow.

The cat came over and wove through Anne's

legs.

Kandi bent down to pet it. "See, it likes you."

"No."

Kandi picked the cat up and set it on the counter. "Poor baby. We're so sorry about your situation. But it'll work out." The cat moved over to Anne, who rubbed its back. The cat began purring loudly.

"Not happening, kitty." Anne reached out and found the small tag around its neck. Minnie.

"Ah, Minnie. Nice to meet you. Now, let's get you some water." Anne went over to the empty saucer and cleaned it before adding some water to the dish. She set it on the floor out of their path and Minnie went over and took a few laps from the saucer.

"She doesn't seem worse for wear. But it's a good thing we came here when we did."

"That's us—sleuths who save cats." Kandi quipped.

"Hmm. Yeah, let me get that printed on some business cards." Anne planted her hands on her hips. "Let's try to figure out how many boxes we need and go get them."

Kandi pulled the notepad from the bag, along with a pen. "Okay, ready to make notes. Can we grab some lunch on the way too? All the sudden I'm in the mood for a tuna sandwich."

The morning went by fairly quickly as they started in the kitchen before making their way to the bedroom. It looked like Laurel was very frugal with her own items and most had seen better days. If that were the case, she wasn't taking the packages for herself, but simply returning them for cash or selling them off to someone else. They'd have to do some digging into that, but it would take time and in reality, it didn't matter anymore. Why Laurel had decided that stealing from others was a good idea had died with her.

After making quick work in the kitchen, items were separated into bags for charity and some items to dispose of. Kandi has also begun a sheet with the list of furnishings. Stewart was going to get a few friends to help him load up the items tomorrow and take them to the thrift store.

They made their way to the bedroom that

Laurel had been using for her office and packing area. Boxes filled pretty much every floor space and the closet also had a few boxes under some shelving that had been added to hold packing material and tape.

In the closet, Anne bent to pick up a box and realized it felt lighter than expected. She lifted it up to find that the bottom had been removed to create a shell. After she pulled it away from its original spot, she spied a dry food dispenser and one for water.

"Ah, no wonder it took some coaxing to get her to come into the kitchen." It was good to know that Minnie had been okay during the short time on her own. That was a relief, and proved what Kandi had thought about Laurel keeping Minnie a secret from the landlord. Anne moved the empty boxes into the living room, where they would collapse any they didn't need. She made her way back to find another large box that had a hole in the side. Sure enough, when she lifted the carton, she found Minnie's litter container.

"Kandi, it looks like Minnie was okay. She had

food and water. However, still good we came when we did."

"Yes, but what's going to happen to her now?" She sniffed.

"Not happening. No." Anne replied.

Kandi showed Anne a list of items ready to go out to buyers. They would take it to the police so they could decide how they wanted to handle it. For now, all those items they stacked on the table against the wall. Back in the kitchen, they made a guess how many boxes they'd need to finish packing the larger items and dishware. There was a box sitting on the kitchen table and Anne picked it up. It was like the other boxes, in that the bottom had been cut off so that it could cover various items.

However, in this case, Anne instantly recognized what she was looking at. It was the basket from Hope's Shoppe. Items were displayed in it. She moved a container from beside a space where something had been before. She bent closer to look at it. It was a piece of something.

"What's that?" Kandi moved to pick it up.

"Stop! Don't touch it."

"Geez, okay." Kandi raised her hands in surrender.

"No, sorry for that. I think I may know what killed Laurel."

"They said it was mushrooms."

"Yes, but she didn't pick them. They were in this basket. I looked at the baskets when I'd dropped by before they had the event. I'm pretty sure that mushrooms weren't included in the items."

"But she could have added the mushrooms later."

"True, but if she had gone out to look for mushrooms, she would have taken all the other items out to use the basket for her foraging."

"Oh, good point." Kandi's eyes grew wide. "This means she was—"

"Murdered."

CHAPTER NINE

Now that they knew Minnie would be okay on her own for a while, they left to go grab lunch. This would give them some time to figure out what to do with her without having to take action right then.

Kandi and Anne drove over to the local café on Main Street since they'd both decided that tuna sandwiches sounded good. After perusing the menu just to see if something else caught their fancy, they both decided to stick with their original thoughts of a tuna salad sandwich on rye bread, some potato salad, and a slice of the delicious Palisade peach pie. Instead of iced tea, they opted for water with a slice of lemon.

Thinking about the wonderful peaches from the Western slope reminded Anne of the fact that she wanted to preserve the peaches when the season returned, and they were in abundance. "Hey Kandi, you ever wonder why they don't say jarring instead of canning?"

Kandi had a puzzled look on her face. "Well, it's because the original term was canister and then over the years it was shortened to canning. So metal, glass, and today even some of those sealed items are most likely the newest form of what we'd call canning. Why are you asking about canning?"

"I want to put up some peaches when they're ready. Last year when I had some in the dead of winter, it was like I'd opened up a can of sunshine." She smiled as the waitress set their sandwiches in front of them, thanking her as the woman said to let her know if they needed anything else.

"Oh, bummer. I should have gone with my first thought." Kandi sighed deeply.

Anne finished with the bite of her potato salad before she replied. "What was that?"

"Potato chips. I was going to get them at first as that's what I was craving, but the potato salad sounded good too."

Anne waved with her hand to get their waitress's attention. "We can't have that. We'll just get an order of chips, too.”

The waitress approached, scanning their plates to see if anything was out of order. “Can I help you?”

“Could we get an order of potato chips please, and if you have any green olives, maybe a few of those as well?”

“Um, sure. I have to get the drinks for that couple but will be back with your items right after that.”

“Great, thanks a bunch.”

Kandi lowered her head and giggled. “She probably thinks we’re kooky.”

“Well, it would be the truth, wouldn’t it?” Anne picked up her sandwich and took a bite.

“I guess so. Thanks. I doubt if I’d have ordered that if you weren’t here. How do you do it?”

Anne pulled a paper napkin from the dispenser on the table and wiped breadcrumbs from her lips.

“Do what?”

“I mean, you just decide you want something

and then you just do it or ask for it."

Anne sat back against the vinyl seat of the booth. "I wasn't always like this. I don't know if it comes with age or if you finally realize you need to speak up for what you want. Either way, as a mother, you'll grow into that, as you'll want to be an advocate for your child. Have you and Stewart started thinking about names?"

"Not really. We're still coming to terms with the fact that we're going to be parents. I'm still wrapping my head around everything." She smiled up as the waitress set down the paper-lined basket of potato chips, along with a small bowl of green olives. Kandi popped one into her mouth. "These hit the spot so much. Thanks for thinking of asking for some of those, too."

After Kandi had finished chewing some potato chips, she took a napkin to her mouth and let out a satisfied sigh. "That was exactly what I needed. Now, back to what we've discovered. Who would have wanted Laurel's death?"

"I'm not sure. Since I didn't know her, or the people she hung around with, it's harder to say.

Plus, we'd have to have some idea of a person's motives for wanting to harm her. Or more importantly, why? Of course, there's also the fact that someone else put those mushrooms into that basket. This is tough because we usually know at least some people that are in someone's life."

Kandi stabbed her fork into the potato salad. "I know who might."

"Who?"

"Sorcha." Kandi popped the potato into her mouth, chewing.

"You think Sorcha could have wanted her dead?"

"No, of course not. I mean, Sorcha tends to have more insights into the comings and goings of the people in this town. She might have some insights into Laurel or her friends."

Upon Anne's move to Carolan Springs, it became clear that Sorcha, a Scottish Sophia Loren, had taken an interest in Sheriff Carson. After Anne and Carson had become an item, the owner of the local bookshop had kept up an amiable relationship with them, but apart from brief pleasantries, they had had little communication with one another. Whether they had tried to avoid one another on purpose, or it was simply that their paths rarely crossed, Anne didn't relish the idea of visiting with the woman after all this time.

"What would you say to the idea of going to ask her what she knows?" Anne bit into the dill pickle, its sour flavor seeming to reflect her current emotions as she thought of an impending conversation with Sorcha.

Kandi held up a potato chip and waved it in Anne's direction. "Nope. You aren't going to put this on me. Plus, then you'll be peppering me with more questions about what she said. We'll go together or not at all."

Anne sighed. "Fine. Now let's finish up so we can go grab those boxes. And I need to decide something important."

"What's that?"

"If I'm going to tell Carson. If he finds out I've gotten involved in possibly another murder, he's not going to be happy with me."

"Well first, tell him. And second, he's going to find out at some point. Better to come from you than from someone else."

Anne's chest rose and then fell as she released a deep and long breath. "It's possible you're right after giving it some thought. Though I would prefer he not think that I was actively seeking trouble."

"Um, didn't you? It's not like we had to go into her house and start nosing around."

"You know, you're not making me feel better." Anne responded.

With a smile, the waitress walked over to their table to top off their glasses with ice cold water. After thanking her, they returned to their conversation.

"I know. It's just, well, you know he hates it when I get involved in these things. But I can't help it. It's not like I go looking for this stuff. It's like sleuthing synchronicity. It just shows up." She shrugged.

"Um, okay. Well, we certainly want to see justice for Laurel if she really was murdered, and it wasn't an accident. Did you, like, grab her journal?"

"Oh shoot. I was going to do that before we left. How about we pick it up when we drop off the boxes? Then I can go home and read it and see if she points the finger to her having issues with anyone."

"Sounds good." Kandi pointed at Anne's plate. "Are you going to eat the rest of your pie?"

Anne couldn't help but laugh as she pushed her partially consumed pie toward Kandi. "Here, mama. You have it."

After paying for lunch, they went in search of the boxes they needed and, once they had them, they drove back to the small house. The living room couch was the ideal spot to place the boxes that were set down. As Anne stared at the box that was on the table, she then remembered the basket that was nearby.

Meow.

Minnie gradually advanced towards Anne, her gaze unwavering as she moved closer. Kneeling down, Anne tenderly wrapped her arms around the cat in a loving embrace before hoisting her up in her arms. "Now look Minnie, don't try to win me over with your sweet, gentle face and those pretty, green eyes. Since you are all alone, why don't you stay with us until we can find a suitable place for you to live? But just so we're clear, I'm not keeping you any longer than necessary."

Minnie nestled in Anne's arms and purred softly in a way that showed her agreement and approval. The cat looked up at her as Anne continued, "However, it's important to know that Mouser may not welcome your entry into his domain."

Anne noticed Kandi trying to conceal her amusement, her lips pressed together tightly in an effort to keep from smiling. "Don't start or you'll be taking her home with you."

"I'm not, like, saying a word."

"Well, yes you are, because that's, um, six right there. Now help me get the food and water dispensers into a box. I'm only taking her home because we can't just leave her here. I don't like the idea of her being alone in case someone comes inside. And we don't have time to go to the rescue right now."

"Okay, sure. I guess you can hold her while I drive."

After setting Minnie on the ground, Anne went into the bedroom in order to fetch the journal. She pondered if there was anything else she should bring along with her. As she spun around, Anne inadvertently caused Laurel's pen to fly off the back of the nightstand.

A sigh of frustration escaped her lips as she said, "Shoot." She contemplated the idea of leaving it, but ultimately decided to get it back just in case it was needed in the future. She tried to peek over the back to grab the pen, but it had fallen so far down that her fingers were too short to reach it. Pulling the nightstand away from the wall, she bent down to retrieve the pen when she noticed a large padded manilla envelope taped to the back of the nightstand. Ripping it from the back, she decided she'd look at the contents at home, along with the journal. She retrieved her pen and pushed the nightstand back to the wall.

She found Kandi in the living room, who had already taken Minnie's items from the house out to the truck. Kandi's mouth opened wide, and she audibly yawned. "I think it's nap time. Let's get Minnie and go home."

"Let's hope that Minnie will do okay on the drive over, since we don't have a crate for her."

"Ah contrary."

"It's not Ah contrary, it's—oh never mind."

Kandi pointed to where Minnie was safely ensconced in a crate, licking her paw.

Anne asked, "Where'd you find that?"

"Front closet."

"Let me guess. Hidden inside a false box?"

"Yep. I figured if she'd hidden everything else relating to Minnie, that she might have a crate somewhere like that, too. Ready?" Kandi picked up the crate and handed it to Anne.

Anne replied. "Yes, let's get you home to nap. Come on Minnie. I can't wait to introduce you to Mouser."

CHAPTER TEN

After they decided to finish collecting boxes and another few errands on the way home, they arrived later in the afternoon. Kandi took off to her home, and Anne made her way back along the drive, her eyes glimpsing the first buds on the Lilac bushes that separated her backyard from that of the Brandywine Inn. She couldn't wait until the bushes were in full bloom as the aroma was lovely and the flowers made wonderful arrangements in the houses.

Anne opened the door to the kitchen and was surprised to see Carson rummaging through the contents of the refrigerator. "Hi you." Upon noticing the carrier, she held in her arms, he came to an abrupt halt. "Would that be what I think it is?"

"Well, yes. And no."

"Ah, so it's Schrodinger's cat then?" He removed a packet of cheese from the refrigerator and placed it on the counter, which already had a plate of crackers and some vegetables on it.

Anne set the carrier down on the table. "Well, yes, it's a cat. But I'm not keeping her. As soon as I find Minnie a home, she's leaving."

He pulled out a slice of cheese and nibbled on it while he leaned against the counter. "You've already named her?"

Anne plopped down in a nearby chair. "No, that's her name. Sadly, her human passed away, and she has no place to go. I recommended the rescue, but Kandi broke down in tears."

"Well, that explains it, then. I mean, you couldn't let Kandi be upset about this cat, now could you?" He winked, and she swatted at him. He deftly moved away from her. "Who owned the cat, and how did you become its provider?"

"Well, don't get mad, okay?" She made a grimace with her mouth.

"Oh, no. I have a feeling I'm not going to like this. Is this another ND issue?" Carson often referred to Anne's sleuthing with the nickname of the famous girl detective Nancy Drew.

"Um, no. Well, yes. But it's not my fault. It's

not like I went looking for a mystery."

"Of course not. They always seem to find you wherever you are. What's the deal? Spill it." He set the plate down on the table before grabbing a glass of iced tea for them both.

Anne shared how she and Kandi were trying to help the parents of Laurel. "We didn't know that she had a cat and, of course, we didn't want to leave it there. But here's the thing—"

"Ah, now we get to the crux of the matter. What did you find?"

Anne thought quickly. She should—she would—tell Carson about the journal and the package she'd found. But she knew him. If she told him she had those items, he'd want them right away to take to the police. Then she may never know what was inside. So, she'd share those items later. It wasn't lying; it was withholding. So that had to be okay, right? Though she felt a check in her spirit, she promptly ignored it, hoping it wasn't going to come back to haunt her.

"Listen, Laurel covered a lot of her items with the bottoms removed from boxes. She may have done that to keep her landlord unaware that she had Minnie. There was one sitting on the kitchen table and when I lifted it up, it was a basket that I'd seen at Hope's."

"Okay?" He crunched on a piece of celery stuffed with hummus.

"The thing is, no mushrooms were included in the other baskets that were given out. So where did the mushrooms come from?" She absently ate some veggies with hummus, even though she wasn't hungry after her recent sandwich.

"Mushrooms?"

"Oh, Kandi told me she learned that she may have died from some mushrooms, but they're still doing tests."

"Between you and Kandi, it's never a dull moment around here."

"Again, I didn't go looking for this stuff. Kandi was the one who found out about it and then let me know."

He crunched on a piece of celery while she spoke about what they'd found. When she finished, he remarked, "She could have set them in the basket."

"That's what Kandi said, but I don't think so. And if she'd have used the basket for foraging, she would have taken out the other items that were in the basket. But again, why go to the trouble to hide it?"

He shrugged. "People have quirks. Even you."

She made a face at his joke. "Yes, but here's the thing. She had a quirk that had her stealing deliveries from people." She picked up a cracker and took a bite out of it, the crumbs falling onto the table. Using her finger, she brushed them up into a pile before dusting them into her hand and dropping them into the nearby trashcan.

"Now that's something new. Have you shared this with the police?"

Anne shook her head. "No, I wanted to talk with you first. Plus, I needed to get Kandi home so she could take a nap. I think this baby is going to really take it out of her. She's normally goes like crazy, but she's been a lot more tired than usual."

"Okay, so let's think about this. She was stealing people's packages. If someone found out—"

Anne bolted in her chair. "Maybe that's what had Hope so upset with Laurel."

"Fill me in here." He rose and went to the fridge to gather more veggies as they'd quickly eaten through the items he'd put on his plate.

"Okay, so Autumn said that when Laurel had come to the mushroom class, she and Hope had been in an argument. Let's see, Hope said something like, you need to quit and then Laurel basically told Hope to mind her own business and blew her off."

"What then?"

"Hope told her something about her short...um, I forget exactly."

Carson's eyebrow rose. "ND? Spill it."

"Well, it makes Hope sound bad, and I know she didn't mean it. Plus, Hope's been avoiding me, and I don't know what's going on with her. I'm worried."

"That just shows you're a good friend. Just so I'm clear, you're saying she had an argument with the victim and now she's left town?"

Anne swallowed. Did that make it even worse? Had Hope left because she knew what could happen to Laurel if she ate those mushrooms? No. If anything, Hope's oath to do no harm meant there was no way she'd even do something to make someone ill. No, Hope hasn't caused the issue. She especially didn't like the fact that he'd noted Laurel was a victim.

"Penny for your thoughts?" Carson asked.

"Well, what if someone saw Laurel stealing a package? But instead of telling the police, they decided to have their revenge?"

"Murdering is pretty strong revenge for seeing someone steal a package that's not even your own."

Anne rose and paced back and forth. "But what if they realized she'd taken their packages too? And what if she'd found something that they didn't want anyone to know about? Certainly, that could be motive."

He showed his agreement by a subtle nod of his head. "It could be true, but it is only an assumption."

"I know. You want the facts." She pulled the chair backwards with a loud screech of its feet against the floor. The sudden motion and sound stirred Minnie awake, causing her to meow to be let out.

"Oh, Minnie, shush. I wanted to introduce you to Mouser later." But Minnie's howl increased. A thump from the front room let them know Mouser had heard the noise. This would be the time they'd learn if the two could get along until she could find Minnie a home.

As Mouser walked into the kitchen, his eyes quickly shifted to the carrier that was positioned there. Minnie's meowing grew louder. Anne glanced over at Carson with a quick look. "What do you think we should do now?"

"Let them look at one another while she's still in the carrier, and then we can check to see if any hissing occurs. If not, then we'll open the door and I'll hold on to Mouser. I don't want you to get scratched if he tries to get to her."

"Okay, sounds like a good plan." Anne set the carrier on the floor and Mouser slunk over to the wired front. Inside, Minnie ceased her howling, and the pair poked their noses at one another. Thankfully, neither hissed, and Mouser's back hairs and tail stayed flat.

Carson went over and scooped up Mouser. "Let's see what happens when you open the door and let her out."

Anne bent down and unlatched the door to the carrier. Minnie stayed inside for a moment before peeking her head out. Upon seeing Anne, she made her way over so that Anne could pet her while a vigilant Mouser watched Minnie from the security of Carson's arms.

Unexpectedly, Carson let out a loud and hearty laugh that echoed through the room.

Anne raised her head and looked up toward him. "What's so funny?"

"Don't you see it? A boy cat named Mouser. And now a girl cat, with all the possible names available, Minnie. You know, like a certain cartoon duo?"

"Oh, I never even thought of that. Though it's not really his name. But you're right, it is funny.

What do you say, we let them meet properly?"

Carson nodded. "All right. But if they go after one another, I'll grab Mouser and you put Minnie back in the carrier. Ready?"

She hesitated, not looking forward to the potential of having to physically intervene and separate two cats if necessary. "Yes." Moving away from Minnie, she pulled the carrier closer to the cabinets, making sure there was enough room available if she needed to grab the calico cat.

"Here we go." Carson set Mouser down on the floor. The pair of cats simply stared at one another, neither of them moving closer or hissing. "Well, at least they're not going after each other right away. What should we do now?"

Anne moved from her position by the carrier and went over to the fridge. She poured a bit of milk into a large saucer and sat it on the floor between the cats. Neither cat moved for a moment. Finally, Minnie slunk over and began drinking from the bowl. Mouser waited a bit before joining her. Before they knew it, the two cats were lapping at the milk side by side.

"I can't believe it. That was too easy." Just as Carson finished speaking, Mouser poked his nose over toward Minnie, who lightly tapped his ear with her paw.

"Hmm, I think Minnie let Mouser know that he was not going to get fresh with her."

He laughed and pulled Anne over into an embrace. "If I get fresh with you, will you promise not to bop me on the ear?"

"Absolutely. Fresh away."

~~

With the cat situation settled for now, and Carson back up in his office typing on his manuscript, Anne sat down with a notepad.

If the mushrooms had been the reason for the young woman's death, then the first thing she needed to find out is who would have that knowledge. She made a note with her pen. Her next thought was about the baskets themselves. Who had delivered the baskets out to people and who had delivered the basket to Laurel? After that, she hit a blank wall with anything else coming to her. She really wanted to look at the package she'd found hidden behind the nightstand and Laurel's journal, but she wanted to wait until Carson was out of the house.

She turned the page in her notebook, writing the words, Why, Who, When, and What. Under what, she added the word, mushrooms. After thinking for a moment, she also added the items of means, motive, and opportunity. She stared at the words on the page. Finally, she decided that the key to this was figuring out who had access to or knowledge about deadly mushrooms.

Obviously, the mycelium's group president most likely was skilled in that area in order to keep the group members safe and had knowledge about the various mushrooms in the area. Additionally, some members of the group would most likely have knowledge as well. But truthfully, anyone who had studied it or did any research could also have the knowledge.

First things first, she needed to speak with the group president.

CHAPTER ELEVEN

Anne devoted the rest of the day to taking care of tasks around the house and making sure that Mouser and Minnie could coexist peacefully. She was comforted when she found them snuggled up together fast asleep in the sunlit spot by the window, calming her anxieties about them being together while she or Carson were gone.

Could it be that Mouser had been feeling lonely, and she hadn't noticed until this point in time? As long as he keeps in mind that Minnie will be heading to her permanent home soon, he should be alright. Maybe she could find some other toys for him. All she knew was that she needed to do something soon before the pair got too attached to one another. Or even worse, her stance on Minnie weakening.

When Carson went off to grab them some burgers for dinner, Anne realized this was her chance to look at the items she'd found at Laurel's. She found her bag and pulled the journal out first.

As the pages fell open, she realized that most were blank. That meant the journal was fairly new then. She opened it to the last page that had some writing on it.

Ugh. Must have some ki— of bug or food poisoning. Not well at all. Going to bed and hoping I'll feel better tomorr—. I need my strength for confronting M— is going to regret messing with me.

Shoot. The letters of the name were smeared, as were others. Laurel may have been crying when she wrote what would be her last words.

This must have been after she'd eaten the mushrooms. Come to think of it, who had found her or called it in? Had Laurel called for help, but it had been too late? That would explain why there were other emergency vehicles that day. As Anne pondered the last hours of the young woman's life, her gaze landed back on the last sentence. Who was she confronting? She didn't know where Laurel worked. If there had been some issues with her employer or other workers, had she sought to address them? Yet, that could also open the door to more suspects in Laurel's death.

After scanning the other entries written in the journal, which were mainly about the events of the day, along with affirmations and quotes, Anne put the journal down on the table.

She slowly and cautiously opened the envelope, carefully undoing the clasp. Inside was another journal and some paperwork. She looked at the paperwork. Looked like items from a temp agency. Scanning through the list, it looked like Laurel had been open to any kind of work, including stocking, retail, dishwashing, cleaning, and delivery service, along with a long list of other items.

Wait a minute. If she had worked for a delivery service, she could have used that to go up on people's porches or decks, leave the items she was supposed to deliver, but take anything else that was there. If anyone looked, it would appear she was just picking up the item for shipping. That was actually a pretty clever way to do it.

After looking through the various documents, nothing stood out. It looked like she may not have had any temp work for a while, though. Anne sat back and thought about it. If Laurel's parents were elderly, chances were that they were on a fixed income. If Laurel had found that it was getting difficult to make enough money to pay her bills, this could explain why she took the packages and sold them. She would need to take some extra time to think this through and get some feedback from Kandi and Hope.

Ahh. Hope. Anne needed to figure out another piece of the puzzle that involved Hope and what else she needed to do to fix their relationship. Her friendship with Hope was too precious to let it slip away. Plus, they were partners in the Inn, even if Hope was the primary owner of the business. But she realized there wasn't much she could do right now if she couldn't get a hold of Hope to find out what was going on. So, there was no point in dwelling on it when she couldn't do anything about it.

After setting the paperwork aside, she opened the journal, which made a slight cracking noise as it opened. The writing within the notebook was like the other journal. However, as she kept reading, the sentences were filled with anger and annoyance, and even the forceful writing style reflected its tone.

I won't put up with it. Treating me like this. After all, we've been through. I didn't mind helping with the plan, but to throw me away like nothing, I won't stand for it. M will regret this.

Anne glanced at the date. A few weeks ago. So, Laurel was dealing with someone who'd wanted her help, but then had stopped the relationship.

Who was M?

And what plan was Laurel willing to help?

~~

The following day, Anne drove over to the police station, saying she'd found the items and didn't know if she could send them to Laurel's parents or if they might be of value in the investigation. They took the items, summarily dismissing her after taking her information.

She left and found herself over at Hope's. Had she returned yet? She stopped in and noticed the shop was emptier than usual for this time of day.

"Hi Autumn. Everyone off hiking?"

Autumn made her stance known by shaking her head. "I'm afraid the answer's most likely no. This day is emblematic of a lot of the days lately around here. This has been the situation for some time now. If I'm being honest, I'm really worried. I want Hope to return soon. I'm at a loss as to what's going on. We have lulls in customers, but this is something different from what I've ever experienced since I've worked here."

"Hope still hasn't returned?"

"No. It's so unlike her. She hasn't even called to check in or anything. I feel something's up though. Even our regular customers haven't been in to shop."

Anne perched on a stool by the counter. "I hate to say it, but do you think that Miranda's place is affecting Hope's Shoppe?"

She shrugged. "Who knows? But it is easy to park and walk to lots of shops whereas here it's not as convenient. Especially with the increased traffic. Even so, we have pickup for orders in the back and, of course, we'll ship to anyone."

"Well, I wish I could help. Hope's not speaking to me either. And I don't know where she is, so that doesn't help, or I'd go and talk to her in person. Anyway, I also stopped by to ask about the president of the mycelium group. I want to find out more about the workshop that day and everyone who attended."

Autumn went behind the counter and pulled up the screen on the computer. "Ah, here it is." She jotted down the woman's name and phone number. Handing the folded paper to Anne, she said, "I heard that Kandi's going to have a baby. So happy for her. If she'd like any info on good herbs for pregnancy, or just to chat about it, I'm here for her."

"That's wonderful. I'm sure she'll take you up on it. See you later." She waved the piece of paper with the president's name on it before heading back out to her car.

It wasn't like Hope to disappear like this, and it had Anne worried even more. If only she knew where she was. She opened the creased note and looked at the name. Marcia Landers. She punched in the number on the phone, but it went to voicemail. Anne left a message and ended the call. Okay, nothing she could do there.

She tapped the steering wheel. Well, if she couldn't speak to Marcia, maybe she could take some time to head over to the garden center. Even though it was still too early to plant, the recent warm, sunny days made it hard not to get the gardening bug. Pulling into the parking lot, she saw that she wasn't the only one that felt that way as people emerged with baskets laden with flowers and veggie starts. Wandering through the greenhouses, she admired all the items and made notes for some of her new clients. Ever since she'd started her garden design business, she'd been able to create wonderful landscapes that were perfect for each individual.

A voice called out to her. "Anne!"

She turned to see a familiar face. "Sam!"

She set down the flat of strawberries, and they embraced in a hug. "It's so good to see you. Looks like marriage suits you."

Anne blushed. "Thanks. And how about you?

Last I heard, you were in DC and things were good with your, um, friend."

"Alas, not meant to be. Our lives were too busy, and to be honest, I missed the mountains. When I got a call to take over for the retiring medical examiner, I decided to head back home."

"Well, we're lucky to have you. But I thought you rented out your place?"

He nodded. "I had, but it's only another month and their lease is up."

"I bet Hank will be happy to get back out there again. How is he?"

"Slowing down. He still thinks he's a puppy, though." He ran his fingers through his thick head of auburn hair.

"Where are you staying if your cabin is occupied?" Anne asked.

"There's a hotel that does month stays. I'm there for now."

Having left her sunglasses in the car, Anne shaded her eyes from the sun. "Well, that won't do. Poor Hank, all cooped up in that place all day. You know you're welcome to stay with us until your house opens back up."

"Thanks. But not sure Carson would go for that." When Anne had moved to Carolan Springs, she'd been dating Sam before she realized her feelings for Carson.

"I think he'd be okay with it. Wait, right now we've been renting out his place, and it will be empty after the next writer's retreat. Why don't you stay there? We can easily make it where Hank can go in and out on his own."

"Really? That would be great." He pulled a card from his wallet. "Here's my number. Talk it over with Carson and let me know. It would certainly be better for Hank and being out in the forest would be good for me, too."

She held up the card. "I'll talk to him today and I'm sure we can work out a good deal on price, too."

"Great. Well, best get back to work. I stopped by here to see about adding some plants to my office. And to grab some flowers for the ladies in the front office. See you later." He turned and walked off, allowing Anne to admire his strong physique, while chiding herself a bit over it. Grabbing up a few packets of seeds and some Dahlia bulbs, she made her way to the checkout counter when her phone rang.

She stepped out of line to answer the call.

"Hello?"

A cheerful, high voice replied. "Hi. This is Miranda. You called me earlier. Sorry to miss your call, but I was out foraging since we'd had that nice rainstorm. I found a wonderful puff ball and some morels. Anyway, how can I help you?"

"I wanted to chat with you a bit about mushrooms and also the class you did at Hope's Herbal Shoppe."

"Okay. Is there any particular reason?"

Anne decided to take the direct approach. "Well, with Laurel dying—"

"What did you say?"

Anne adjusted the phone against her shoulder as she shifted her items to the other arm. "I'm sorry. I thought you knew."

"No. What happened? Was she in an accident?"

"Um, it seems she ate some poison mushrooms."

The line went quiet. Anne thought the call had dropped. "Hello?"

"No, I'm here. Just in shock. But there's no way that Laurel would have eaten mushrooms without strong verification or provenance. It must have been something else."

Anne didn't want to argue with the woman, as she was afraid she might not continue talking to her. "That's why I'd like to speak with you about it. Could we meet as it would be much easier than a phone call?"

"I suppose. I can't do it today. Let's meet, um, Tuesday. I have a talk at the bookstore I'm prepping for right now. Once it's over, then we can grab some coffee."

"Sounds good. What's your talk about?"

There was hesitation on the line before Marcia replied.

"Mushrooms and Murder."

CHAPTER TWELVE

After a bit more conversation, Anne was reminded of the scrumptious pastries on display in the French Bistro and put forward the idea to Miranda that they should meet there. As the patio was filled with guests, they took a seat inside. The restaurant seemed to be a success, judging from its full capacity. As a tall and thin woman dressed in navy blue slacks and wearing a freshly pressed white shirt came over to take their drink order, they looked over the menu. When she got back with their lattes, Anne decided to have a Pain au Chocolat while Marcia chose a delicious sounding Almond Croissant.

Anne noted the woman with a no-nonsense pixie haircut that framed her pretty face. Large blue eyes were the perfect compliment to her light skin, now brushed with a hint of sunburn, so often seen when people forgot about Colorado's high altitude and the sun's rays. She wore the typical Colorado uniform of trail pants with lots of pockets, a rose top with cutouts for thumb holes, and a pair of name-brand trail runners. Her outfit was completed with a much-loved canvas messenger bag. Anne immediately liked her.

Marcia took a sip of the latte and sighed. "This is delightful. I hadn't been in yet, so thanks for suggesting we meet here."

"My pleasure. And thanks for meeting with me. How'd your talk go?" Anne held the unusual cup, which had two handles, and took a drink of the latte.

"Great. Turns out that subject brought in a lot of curious people. The place was packed. Thanks for asking. Hopefully, it will help people to learn more about mushrooms and they won't get such a bad rap."

Anne nodded. "I think my favorite are portobellos. But I have to admit, I don't know much about mushrooms either. Basically, I stick with oyster or baby bellas if I buy any from the store." She steered the conversation back to her intent for their meeting. "It sounded like you were really surprised about Laurel."

Marcia set her cup in the saucer before scooting her chair closer to the table. "Yes, well, first let me say that I didn't know her well. In fact, it's only been probably a month since she joined the club. The fact is, you may have people join to attend one meeting and then you never see or hear from them again. She had been to a meeting and was scheduled to join our upcoming foraging outing, but she had shared that she wanted to learn because she didn't want to make the mistake of picking the wrong ones. That's why when you said they believe that caused her death, I couldn't believe it."

Had Anne said that? She tried to remember but thought that she'd only said Laurel had possibly died from the mushrooms. However, it probably stood to reason that she would have had to get that information from someone. Anne remembered that she'd taken a picture of the mushroom in the basket they'd found at Laurel's. "I have a picture of a mushroom. Would you be able to identify it if you saw it? It's a picture on my phone."

"I may be able to give you an idea, but without seeing it in person and noting the gills, etc. I couldn't tell you definitively."

"That's okay. I'd just like your basic opinion."

"Sure." Miranda said.

Anne dug her phone out and pulled up the picture she'd taken. She passed it over to Miranda, who concentrated on the picture. Quiet for a while, Miranda finally spoke. "Don't quote me on it, but it looks like an Amanita Fatalis."

"Is that deadly?" Anne asked.

"Yes. Where did you find it?"

At that moment, her phone beeped. "Excuse me. I'm waiting on a message from my husband."

It was a message from Carson, noting that the police had released the house for her and Kandi to finish their packing. She hadn't thought of them locking the place down again, but it had made sense after she brought them the journals and told them about the basket with the hidden mushroom. It had made sense that they would want to go back to ensure that nothing had been overlooked. Unfortunately, they hadn't been happy with them for going into the house, but Anne had made sure that Carson informed them that the landlord had given them the all-clear. Plus, it wasn't her fault they hadn't done their due diligence to begin with. One thing she knew, it was a good thing she'd grabbed Minnie when she had the chance, as they had taken more than a week to allow the landlord to do anything else with it.

She put her phone back in her purse.

"Sorry, I'd been expecting that text."

"Isn't that the way with technology now? We live our lives around it instead of allowing our lives to use it as needed."

"I guess. I mean, you have a cell phone, don't you?"

"Yes. It's currently at my house." She smiled as the waitress set the croissant in front of her and the pastry in front of Anne.

Anne thanked the waitress before continuing. "So, you don't carry it with you?"

"No. I lived much of my life without carrying

it with me and unless I'm taking a trip or headed out of town, I just leave it at home and return the calls and texts at my convenience. I worked in the tech industry for many years and now it's my time to have some space from it."

Anne stared at Miranda, trying to figure out her age. She appeared to be young, but her attitude was that of someone older.

"I see a confused look on your face. I'll put you out of your misery. Forty-seven."

"What? No way!"

Miranda shrugged. "I've always looked young for my age and some years back I helped mother nature along when I still worked at a tech firm. When I decided to retire, well, let's just say that I don't have to work any more if I don't want to."

Anne took a drink of her coffee, letting this information percolate. Miranda was evidently a smart and successful woman. Therefore, it would be doubtful that she would have needed Laurel's help with anything. But the problem was that she didn't know what the plan entailed, so that was no help. Finally, she spoke. "Well, you look great."

"Stress tends to age you as well. Once I removed that and started getting out in nature more, I felt it resonate with me. I feel like I'm aging backwards sometimes." Her brilliant smile made Anne respond in kind.

"Whatever it is, I need some of that youth elixir. Is that why you started the mycelium group?"

"Partly. I had to decide what I wanted to do with this one crazy life and settled on the fact that I wanted to spend my time learning about healing. A lot of study led me to mycelium and how it's so important to our world. It's an important piece of our ecology. From there I began growing edible mushrooms and soon people started to want to buy them from me or learn how to grow their own. Before long I'd expanded and now, I even sell to restaurants like this one."

"You've sold them mushrooms?"

"Not yet. But they have an order with me for an upcoming bloom."

"Bloom?"

Marcia replied, "Yes. I'm not sure if you know

but the mushroom that you and I see and eat is actually the bloom of mycelium. The rain or snow and other weather events supply the right conditions for blooming."

"I never knew that. That's very interesting." Anne took another sip of her latte before continuing. "When we spoke, you said you had done a talk on mushrooms and murder. Had you done that talk before or had you done others like it? I'm just curious as I know that Laurel attended the meeting at the Herbal Shoppe."

Marcia cocked her head and tapped her fingers against her lips, trying to recall the time. "Sorry, to be honest, I don't recall if she was there or not. As you can imagine, it got many people wanting to hear it that talk. That's why we did it again. We held it in conjunction with the library."

Anne perked up at that. "You mean Sorcha's place?"

"Ah, do you know Sorcha?"

"Yes, I mean we're acquaintances since I've moved here. I've been busy with first running a bed-and-breakfast and then last year starting my gardening design business."

Marcia grinned. "That's not all I've heard about you. Seems like you've gotten into some other things, too."

Anne shrugged her shoulders, knowing exactly what Marcia was referring to. "I don't go looking for things, they just show up for me."

Marcia lowered her voice. "May I give you a word of advice?"

"Um, sure." Anne brushed away any crumbs that had settled on the corner of her mouth.

"No matter how much you play with fire and think you're safe, one day you're going to get burned. Sometimes it's best to stay out of its path."

Anne sat back in silence. Was this a friendly gesture by someone or a word of warning? Either way, she felt a knot in her gut at the words to 'stay out of the way.'

Marcia either ignored Anne's reaction or quickly went back to the subject at hand. "I had stopped in at Sorcha's and asked about hosting our next group meeting. We often meet at different locations so that people can also support local businesses. Just like we did at your friend, Hope's place."

"Okay. But if you don't think that Laurel collected those mushrooms herself, I wonder how she got them."

"She was interested in them, but was concerned about picking the wrong ones. That's why she was keen to attend our next foraging foray. For her to be that hesitant and she wasn't even sure she'd try the ones we found, I can't see her taking it on herself to go out, find some mushrooms and then cook them up. We have people work with experienced guides and there are a lot of tests we do about the mushrooms."

That piqued Anne's interest. "Like what?" She sighed with contentment, wishing her plate held more than the detritus of pastry crumbs. Their waitress brought their bill, and it was difficult not to ask for some goodies to go.

Marcia gestured with her hands. "Well, of course, the first thing we look at is sight. What the mushroom looks like, especially the gills and the stem areas. Then there's the paper test."

"Paper test?"

"Yes, the top is removed from the stem, and it's laid on a piece of paper. Basically, it's a stamp impression of the head. There's more, but I won't bore you with it. You should really come out with us and join us on a foray. If you enjoy getting out in the forest, you'll be amazed at the things we discover when you're focused."

"I might just take you up on your offer. It certainly isn't boring to me. I wouldn't mind growing some basic oysters for use at home."

"I definitely have some of those that will be ready soon. They're really easy to do and you can get a few flushes out of them. Then when you're done, just use the growing medium as another addition to your compost pile and even your garden. I've known some people to have mushrooms come up from doing that as well."

"How fun. Is it a lot of work?" Anne laid some cash on the table, and Marcia handed her card to the waitress, who returned quickly.

"Not at all. Basically, spritzing them with

some water. Then next thing you know, they're taking off."

"Okay, you've sold me. Well, as much as I hate to quit this conversation, I've got to get going. But thanks for meeting with me." Anne rose from her seat and Marcia followed suit.

"You're welcome." They walked toward the entrance when Marcia touched Anne on the arm. "Seriously, come get a mushroom kit and come out on a foray. I see someone I know, so I'll say goodbye here."

"Okay. Will do. Thanks." Anne watched as Marcia headed over to the group of waiters in the corner. One looked familiar. Oh yes, he was the handsome one that had waited on her and Kandi the other day. She smiled as the hostess bid her good day in French, exiting the building into bright sunlight.

After slipping on her sunglasses, Anne pulled her phone out and texted Kandi to see if she was ready to do more packing. She headed to the car when she heard the ping of a return text on her phone.

I can be there in about fifteen minutes.

After acknowledging Kandi's text, she headed toward her car, and on the way passed two women, their heads bent in conversation. Anne's ears perked at what she heard.

"When I was growing up, they used to call her mother a witch."

"You don't say." The woman exclaimed.

"Who knows what she passed on to her daughter? And even worse, it makes me a bit concerned about what she's putting in her tinctures and other items."

They had to be speaking about Hope. But she had to be sure. Forcing herself to remain calm, she hurried over to the ladies, trying to appear similar in her demeanor. "I'm sorry to intrude. But I couldn't help overhearing. I just want to make sure that I'm not buying items from a place that...well, you know."

The women's eyes widened, as big and round as saucers. "It's the Herbal Shoppe on Main Street."

With a look of eagerness and excitement, the

woman leaned in closer. "Nooo. I thought it was owned by a doctor."

"According to her, that's the story, anyway. How are we to know if what she says is true?" Her face showed an air of superiority as she asked her question.

Anne bit her tongue. She wondered if this is how the people had started all the false accusations back during the witch trials. She fought the urge to give them a good dressing down. That wouldn't help her find out what people were saying in order to help Hope.

"Exactly. I wish there was some way I could find out more about this. And I wonder who I can trust to get the items I need now." She acted as if she agreed with them, but she wanted to ring the other woman's neck for her lies about Hope.

The woman bent closer. "You should check out the new place. Miranda's."

"Oh, really? I haven't heard of it."

"Yes, it's fantastic, and the pricing is less than the Herbal Shoppe, too. While they don't have exactly the same things, they're planning on adding new items to their stock if enough people request it."

Ah, that explained it. Miranda was undercutting her prices to be less than Hope's, and finding out what items were selling before she stocked them. With the rumors and beating Hope's prices, it could deter people from buying from the Shoppe. She forced herself not to give the women a piece of her mind. Instead, she pasted on a fake smile and replied to the women. "Like you, I want to make sure that my money is going to a good establishment. So you found all this out through..."

The woman took a moment to survey the area before bending in closer to speak in a hushed voice, "My friend was the one who gave me this information. I generally try to refrain from gossiping, however, did you hear that there was an unfortunate tragedy that befell someone who attended an event at her store? I heard she died."

One woman gasped. "No!"

The woman nodded and continued, "And it was right after the owner had been fighting with her. Who knows, maybe she put a spell on her!"

The other woman tittered at this statement. "Oh, my."

Anne knew she had to get away before she did or said something she'd regret. They'd be calling her more than a witch if she responded. "Thanks for letting me know." She strode away from the gossips, her fists clenched in anger. Someone was spreading rumors about Hope and her shop. If she didn't know better, she felt it was most likely Miranda trying to pull people away from Hope's Shoppe. She would have most likely heard about Hope and Laurel's fight in front of everyone. Certainly, she could have blown that out of proportion as well. But that left Anne wondering if Miranda would go so far as to killing someone to stop a competitor.

CHAPTER THIRTEEN

Anne and Kandi were able to make quick work of the rest of the house. They bundled up a couple of boxes of the young woman's items, taking them over to be mailed to the parents. Arriving at the post office, Anne had to leave Kandi in the truck, who'd broken down sobbing about the poor young woman. Anne knew women who were pregnant often had moody days, but before, Kandi had seemed so excited about having this baby. Now there was an invisible cloud that hung over her and she'd been unusually quiet as they had completed the work.

Dropping Kandi back at her house, she took her time ensuring no kids were out riding their bikes in the cul-de-sac. She'd learned to be extra careful now that little children could be in her path as she backed out of her driveway. Carson had even recommended they back into the driveway, so they'd be facing out as they left the house. It would take some getting used to doing it, but certainly would cut down on any stress because of her worrying about not being able to spot one of the children playing.

Anne waved at her new neighbor as the woman kneeled in her yard, cleaning out a flower bed for planting. She'd wondered about a housewarming gift. Maybe some bulbs or flowers would work. She'd need to take a detour over to the garden center and look around before heading back into town.

Pulling out of the cul-de-sac, she headed toward town. Without Hope to bounce ideas off, she had to find out about the meeting at the library. And that meant speaking to Sorcha. Better to get it over sooner than later.

She parked down from the bookstore and made her way to the front, where she admired the window display. With Sorcha's daughter off at college, the display hadn't been changed yet. It must have been the one that had been set up for the Murder and Mushrooms meeting, as it was a combination of nonfiction books about mycelium, along with some cookbooks and some fiction.

Entering the store, Anne took a moment for her vision to adjust to the dimly lit room, and when it did, she spotted Sorcha with a customer. Sorcha looked as captivating as ever in her heather green dress, with a wide brown leather belt slung low against her hips, exuding her usual magnetism. She had on her suede tan boots and her hair, a vivid red, was left cascading down her back in soft, flowing waves.

Sorcha momentarily looked away from her task and spoke, "I won't keep you waiting for long, I'll be right with you." Glancing over, she saw Anne and gave her a friendly smile.

Anne replied with a small wave of her hand, "Take all the time you need, there is no rush. I'm just browsing and looking at what's available."

Sorcha gave a nod in agreement and guided the women to the counter, where she began to ring up a pile of books.

After the woman had departed, Sorcha made her way across the store to the section where Anne was looking through the books about Colorado's perennial plants. "Well, hello. It's good to see you.

Although I could ask 'where are you keeping yourself?', but I already have a good idea of the answer."

She smiled widely and then leaned over to give Anne a few air kisses. After exchanging greetings, Anne began to realize that her previous opinion of Sorcha may have been incorrect. Even though Anne and Sorcha both had been mutually attracted to Carson, it was Anne that had captured his heart. Though, truth be told, Anne had not returned to the bookstore because she felt inadequate compared to Sorcha's stunning looks. She questioned whether her actions had been the root cause of the ongoing animosity between them all those months ago.

"I'm sorry. I've been busy. But that's no excuse. How's Melissa doing at school?"

"She loves it. And of course, I hate it!" The mood was instantly lightened as Anne joined in, creating an atmosphere of laughter and joy. "Is there a possibility we could take some time out of our busy schedules for a cup of coffee, and then you can explain why you're really here?" With a gentle gesture, Sorcha carefully removed any trace of a flaw from her perfectly shaped lips.

Without hesitation, Anne replied, "Sure. I'd like that."

"Okay, let me get Tom to watch the front and we can go out to the back unless you'd like to stay inside."

Anne replied, "Outside sounds wonderful."

"Excellent. I won't be gone for long." Sorcha made her way to the back of the room, and Anne could hear her talking. There was a reply to the sound, the voice being deep and distinctly masculine. Sorcha re-emerged and enveloped Anne in a warm embrace, her arms encircling Anne's left arm. "Now is the perfect time to get up to speed on where we have been. It feels like an age has gone by since the last time we spoke."

As Sorcha and Anne proceeded towards the kitchen, Sorcha released her hold on Anne's arm. With her hands full of various cups, as well as a plate of delicious looking buttery-pecan cookies, Sorcha pushed open the back door with her hip to uncover a secluded area which was furnished with a sofa and a few chairs, plus a table that was in a sunny spot of the garden. The sweet aroma of jasmine filled the atmosphere, wafting through the air. "Here we are. Would you like to take a seat on the sofa, or would you rather take your seat at the table?"

The sofa had brightly patterned cushions that were most likely warmed from the sun's rays. "Sofa sounds good."

"Terrific. The sofa and chairs would have been my first choice, too." Sorcha carefully placed the tray on the wrought iron coffee table, before offering a cup of the beverage to Anne. "Sandie?" Reaching out with the tray of delicious cookies, she offered them to Anne.

"Even though I know I shouldn't, these treats look so delicious that I can't help but be tempted." Biting off a small piece, she sampled one of the mouthwatering, crispy, melt-in-your-mouth confection.. "Oh, this is wonderful."

"I should say thank you and take credit for these delicious treats, but they were actually purchased from the recently opened bakery on

Market Street." Sorcha added some extra flavor to her coffee before making herself comfortable and leaning back into the chair. "I'm curious to know what the actual purpose of your visit is?"

"I'd like to hear your opinion on Market Street before I give you my response. Do you think it's taking business away from shops on Main Street?"

With carefulness, Sorcha set her cup down on the table, and then she smoothed out her dress. "At the beginning, I was apprehensive, but then I realized that we all have the same goal in mind; to have all businesses do well." She paused, reluctant to reveal her opinion, but then continued. "It may be easier for me not to be worried since there's no other bookstore. But I don't think it should harm other businesses. Rising tide and all that. However, is it because you're wondering how Miranda's place might potentially affect the business at Hope's Herbal Shoppe?"

Anne shifted in her seat, enjoying the warmth against her back. "To be completely honest, the answer is yes. In addition, I've encountered some unpleasant gossip regarding Hope. This most recent event in which a young woman passed away after an event at the Shoppe isn't helping matters either."

"I heard about that. Such a heartbreaking tragedy to have a life, especially one so young, end so abruptly. But I don't know why that would affect Hope's business. Having been in this town for quite some time, she's well known and highly respected by the people here." Sorcha lifted her coffee mug, which was monogrammed with the store's initials, and took another sip from it.

"Without a doubt, that statement's indeed true. The possibility of that had not occurred to me." Anne was determined to put an end to the tension that had been in the air, so she took a deep breath. "Listen, I need to get something off my chest."

"O...kay." Sorcha tilted her head to hear more clearly what was being said.

"I'm going to be upfront about it, so please give me a moment." With her hands tightly intertwined, Anne gathered her courage in order to speak her mind. "When I first arrived here, I must admit that I was a bit intimidated by you."

"What? Intimidated by me?" Her features seemed to register the surprise she felt at that moment. "Why ever for?"

Anne made a gesture towards her with her free hand. "Well, I mean, look at you. You're drop dead gorgeous for starters."

Sorcha let out a loud, hearty laugh and threw her head back in amusement. "You've just made my day. I find it very flattering that you think I'm gorgeous. You must have noticed the makeup I'm wearing, and this hair color has been especially enhanced over the last few years, I can assure you. Plus—"

Anne quickly raised her hand in an attempt to stop Sorcha from continuing her response. "I stand by my word. I truly believe you are a beautiful woman, and I didn't think I had a chance with Carson compared to you. I mean, look at me."

Sorcha adjusted her posture, so that she was

sitting upright and forward in her seat. "Honesty is the best policy, so I want to let you know that I felt I couldn't compete with you."

"What?" Anne was so taken aback by Sorcha's unexpected words that she found herself unable to respond.

"Yes, you are naturally pretty. From the moment we encountered one another, it was clear that you possess an impressive wit and an astute mind. As the expression goes, you've got the whole package, the whole enchilada."

Anne shook her head, chuckling to herself. "I can't believe this. We were each thinking the other ...oh, it boggles the mind."

"Well, think about it. Carson was in a really unfortunate situation. Two women had become interested in him and were vying for his affections. He'd didn't have a chance."

Anne said, "I didn't—"

Sorcha's expression changed to one of disapproval as her eyebrow rose in a perfect arch.

The color rose in Anne's cheeks. "I suppose I had some level of interest in him, okay? Not immediately, however."

"The thing is, the heart is driven by what it truly desires. There was never any kind of contest between us, no matter how small. After the homesteader's fair, when I observed Carson gazing at you, I quickly realized that he was a lost cause. No matter how much you try to hide it, your face will always give away your true emotions when your heart's involved." As Sorcha reclined in her chair, a tranquil quietness enveloped the two of them.

Anne's arms fell heavily to her knees, and she felt tears begin to well up in her eyes. Embarrassed at her display, she quickly pulled herself together. But it was too late. Sorcha moved towards the couch and sat down right beside Anne. "What seems to be the trouble? I'd have thought that my response would have made you happy, not sad."

Anne sought to suppress her emotions, yet her hands gave her away as she gripped them in her lap. "I'm sorry. I'm just worried about Hope, and Kandi's expecting and that's going to change their lives, and I don't know. I'm feeling so confused and I don't know what my next step should be."

"Yes, I understand what you're saying. I'm not immune to questioning and feeling out of sorts. For instance, in light of Melissa leaving for college, do I still have the desire to keep the bookshop going? I'm having difficulty deciding whether to stay in this town or start a new journey and possibly travel to Scotland. Whenever our lives undergo substantial changes, inevitably, it will affect us and make us wonder if we have made the right decisions. When the people we love have their lives change, it can't help but affect us too. Now, let's focus on one thing at a time. Could you elaborate on why you are so worried about Hope? Let's start there."

Anne licked her lips and loosened the tight grip of her hands, running them up and down her legs to release some tension. "Ever since she left a while ago, I've been unable to reach her through calls or texts, and I don't know where she is. I've been trying to think back if there is anything I said or did that may have caused her to become upset. I'm completely at a loss for ideas, and nothing comes to mind. I'm concerned that these rumors could cause damage to her business, and I worry that she's not here to address them. The reason I visited you initially was for that purpose. You recently hosted an event here for the mushroom club."

Sorcha moved back to the adjacent chair to allow easier conversation. "Yes, I can confirm that. Marcia proposed hosting an event about mushrooms, and I offered our venue as a possible location for the gathering. Taking this evening approach has occasionally generated a few sales in the past."

Anne eyed the cookies but stopped herself from taking another one. "Was the theme her idea?"

Sorcha poured fresh, hot coffee into both their cups. "No. I came up with that, as I knew that would draw more people in."

"Did it work?"

Sorcha responded with a quick nod of her

head. "Almost too well. I was forced to close the doors because the space was filled to capacity. Standing room only. Marcia and I were so pleased with the outcome, so we recently did it again. We're also thinking that we might try it again in a few months."

Anne listened intently. "Do you know if Laurel was present for the first presentation?

Sorcha pursed her lips and thought. "Hmm. There were so many people. I guess she could have been. Why do you ask?"

"Well, it was the following week she died from eating poisoned mushrooms."

An expression of dismay came over Sorcha's face as she uttered the words, "Oh no. I was completely unaware of the fact that's what had occurred. This is news to me." Sorcha had a look of concentration on her face as she sipped her coffee.

"That's why I wondered if she'd been here. What about Miranda? Did she attend?"

"Yes, I remember her coming in. She had a little entourage of a few people with her. Did you know that Miranda used to live here before—when she was young?"

Anne crossed her legs before laying her hands in her lap. "What? No. I didn't know that."

"Yes, she grew up here. Don't say I told you, but I think she's always been a bit of a bully. If she didn't get her way, then watch out. From what I've heard, people who went to school with her were glad when she moved away."

"I wonder why she decided to move back here, then? Doesn't sound like any love lost between her and others."

"Well, that was, let me see, about twenty, maybe more, years ago. Her father died not too long ago and left her their place up on old Creek Road. I think at first she meant to come back simply to clear it out and sell it but decided to stay put after going through a recent divorce. Which probably isn't surprising if what I've heard about the way she treats people."

"Old Creek Road? Isn't that the huge house you can see when you up on the mountain in the distance?"

Sorcha nodded. "The one and only."

"Which then begs another question. If she has money, why open up something that competes with Hope? It sounds like it's not like she needs it."

"They both attended the same school together and were classmates during their time there. Hope was the only one who had the courage to confront her about her bullying behavior. She put Miranda in her place in front of everyone. As you can imagine, that didn't go over too well. Lots of stuff started happening, like things in her locker or rumors about her, but Hope was the better person. She refused to get drawn into it. She'd said what she wanted to say, and that was that." Sorcha took her cup from the table and put it back in the tray.

That stopped Anne. "Really? I've never seen Hope be confrontational. Though she had a similar occurrence recently."

"I know you've become friends with Hope since you've moved here. But I've known her pretty much of my life and she has a steel backbone when she needs it."

The memory of her scolding Anne came to the forefront of her thoughts. Don't I know it, she thought. Hope and Miranda not only knew each other, they had been enemies in school.

Something nibbled at Anne's subconscious, but it wouldn't come to the surface. "Do you have the list of the people who attended the event? If you don't mind, I'd like to take a look at it."

"Sure. Follow me." Sorcha walked ahead of Anne, back into the bookstore. She pulled up a ledger where everyone had signed up for the talk. Running her finger down the page, Anne noticed some familiar and some unfamiliar names, couples, and individuals. Her finger stopped as she landed on a name.

Hope's.

"Hope attended the talk?"

"Yes. She was giving out a basket as a raffle prize, and if anyone else wanted one, they could order it from her. I bought one too. I loved the basket, plus it had lots of goodies in it—bath bombs, some floral or herbal sprays, and the big prize had a few mushroom books in it as well."

"Did it have fresh mushrooms?"

"No. Just packaged products." Sorcha set the book back under the counter. "Why?"

"Just curious. Who won the basket?"

"Who else? Miranda."

Anne thought hard. "Did Miranda take the basket with her?"

"No. There were some items that hadn't been added to it. It was going to be delivered the following day."

"Oh, did you deliver it, then?"

"No. As far as I know, Hope did."

Anne thanked Sorcha for the coffee and cookies, saying they needed to get together for lunch in the future. Sorcha also noted that, as grown women, they shouldn't be so hard on themselves. "It seems like we're our own worst enemies."

Anne agreed, noting why it was so easy to focus on our flaws instead of our uniqueness and personal beauty. Sorcha was drawn away to help with a customer, so Anne bid her goodbye. She walked out into the sunlight, but a shiver found its way up her spine. Laurel had attended the mushroom presentation, as had Miranda and Hope. With Miranda winning the basket, another thought occurred to her. If Hope had delivered the basket to Miranda and simply left it, had Laurel later stolen it? One thought played in her mind. If that had been the case, it could only mean one thing.

Had Miranda been the intended victim?

CHAPTER FOURTEEN

As Anne made her way home, her head was a jumble of ideas and emotions. Miranda and Hope had been acquainted since they attended high school, and Hope had been courageous enough to confront her. The fact that Miranda chose to open her own shop, intending to compete with Hope's was a clear sign that she was out for revenge. Without a doubt, Hope would never intentionally do anything to hurt the woman, yet just the fact that she had returned to the town and opened an apothecary must have been extremely distressing for Hope.

Maybe that was the cause of her temporary departure from the town. She most likely had wanted to take some time to think about the situation without other distractions. While Anne had a habit of leaping into something with little thought, Hope was much more likely to take some time to think things through before making a move. The contradictions, along with the similarities between them, had forged a strong bond of friendship and a successful business venture.

As Anne entered her home, she was welcomed by the savory aroma of garlic and butter sizzling in a pan, luring her towards the kitchen.

Something smells absolutely amazing.

She pushed the door open, and her eyes immediately fell upon the kitchen table. There was one of Hope's baskets. She swiveled her body around to face the stove. Mushrooms.

She switched off the stove and then quickly chucked the mushrooms into the garbage right as Carson walked into the kitchen. "What are you doing?"

"The mushrooms. Poisonous." She pointed at the basket.

"No, they're not. I went shopping at the grocery store and bought them. All the conversation about mushrooms sparked an appetite for them on top of some creamy garlic pasta. I knew you've been busy, so I thought I'd take care of dinner."

Anne's shoulders slumped as she slid down into the chair, cradling her head in her hands. "I'm sorry. What an idiot."

"Sweetie. Do you want to talk about what's wrong?" He reached down, gently lifting her up and then placed her head against his chest in a tender embrace. She felt a sense of calm wash over her as she felt the steady rhythm of his heartbeat against her ear.

"I saw the basket, and I thought—"

"Autumn brought it by. She indicated that Hope had desired for you to have one for yourself."

"And it didn't have any mushrooms in it?"

"No." His lips pressed gently against her face. "Honey, I'm worried about you. There is much more to this than just mushrooms. Could you tell me what this is about?"

"I'm worried about Hope and it's sounding more and more like Miranda is trying to shut down Hope's shoppe. And Kandi's going to have a baby. Their lives are changing, our lives are changing. I'm feeling a little off balance and I can't quite put my finger on it."

His immense hand gently encased hers as Carson took her hand in his. "Come on. Let's go outside and get some fresh air and sit for a while."

"I'm sorry about the mushrooms. That smelled so good. I've caused the destruction of what would have been a delectable meal."

"That's okay. But now you're going to owe me supper out." He winked.

"Fine. We could go to that new French place if you'd like. I bet they have mushrooms on the menu."

He pointed at her. "Okay, but your treat."

She laughed. "Certainly, I'll gladly do that." She leaned in and planted a gentle kiss on him as they settled into the porch swing. For a while they just rocked back and forth, gradually allowing the tension to dissipate from her neck and shoulders. After contemplating in silence, she finally broke the quiet with her words. "How should I handle the situation I'm facing with Hope?"

"Put your mind at ease and don't worry. When Hope's ready to talk, she'll let you know. I know she cherishes your friendship. It's likely that there is something else entirely different at play here."

"Could be. Did you know that she went to school with Miranda? The lady who owns the new apothecary?"

"I was already away at school during that time."

She grinned at him. "Oh, yeah. I forgot you're old."

"Funny." He tapped her nose with his finger.

Rather than visiting the restaurant that night, Carson and Anne opted to stay in for the evening. After Carson headed out to grab a pizza, Anne made her way to check on Kandi. Anne found her and Stewart upstairs in the room that was going to be used as the nursery, removing items so they could paint and renovate it. After inviting them over for pizza, Stewart left to call Carson and ask him to pick up a couple more pizzas, one of which should have extra green olives, per Kandi's request.

Anne shared some of her visit with Sorcha at

the bookstore with Kandi.

"See! I told you she liked you. You just wouldn't listen to me."

"Okay. Rub it in. Listen, now that it's confirmed, I'd like to do a celebration lunch, baby shower for you. I was thinking of having it at the French Bistro. What do you think?"

"That sounds wonderful."

"Great. At this moment, is there anything I can do to help?"

Kandi shook her head. "No. But I hope they hurry up with that pizza. I'm starving."

"Is that any different from any other time?"

"No." Kandi giggled. "Let's go over to your house before Carson gets back and pick out a movie."

"Okay."

Kandi ventured into Anne's kitchen, inhaling the delightful aromas that were present in the air. "Oh, wow. It smells so good here. What is it?"

"Sadly, it 'was' dinner until I threw it in the garbage."

"Why would you, like, do that?"

"It was mushrooms."

Kandi's sides were shaking with laughter, and she bent over in response. "Oh no. What was Carson's reaction when you threw it away in the trash can?"

"Thankfully, nothing. I'm truly blessed to have found a man who is so patient in dealing with some of the less desirable aspects of me. Like thinking everyone and everything is suspect."

"I think you both won out. And I'm glad you both finally admitted how much you mean to one another."

Anne held her hands up. "I've already surrendered. No need to stick the knife in twice."

The distinct sound of a cat's feet padding against the floor caused them to pivot their heads towards the front room. Kandi crouched down as she noticed Minnie making her way towards her, with Mouser faithfully trailing behind. "Oh, hey, there Minnie. Do you remember me?"

The cat snuggled up in her arms and purred contentedly. "Ah, you love it here, don't you? Mouser, from the looks of it, you have made a new friend, am I right?"

"Kandi, enough. You're like cut glass—you're so transparent."

Kandi let out a little laugh, a giggle of delight. "Now, you said you'll tell me more about your visit later. So, what else did you uncover when you went to Sorcha's? I'm ready to hear what you found out."

Anne reflected on the words that Sorcha had expressed. "Now think about it. We have Laurel, who we know was a porch pirate. We have a delivery up to Miranda's by Hope."

After Kandi placed Minnie back on the floor, the two cats ran back into the other room. "But Hope wouldn't have put poisoned mushrooms in the basket. Wait, M. Do you think that Marcia also had an issue with Miranda? Aren't they the same age?"

"Hmm. I think Marcia is older or younger than Miranda, but probably not by much. I guess it could be a possibility. But I would think the last thing you'd want to do is include something that could point directly back at you."

"But it wouldn't. Let's say that Hope, like, took the basket up to Miranda's, then Marcia came later and stuck the mushrooms in the basket. Only for Laurel to come along and grab the basket."

"That's a lot of everything fitting neatly together. Though it's not out of the realm of possibility. Also, wouldn't that big mansion have cameras? That would ruin her alibi." Anne pulled out plates to use for the pizza.

Kandi pulled napkins from a drawer and placed them on the table. "Hmm. That's a good point. We should go up there and speak to Miranda."

"No, 'we' are not doing anything of the sort. I don't want you overdoing it."

"This isn't the middle ages. I know women who do all kinds of things right up until they have their babies."

"Sure. But they aren't ones that I love and want to make sure stay healthy. Please make sure that you're taking care of yourself and not pushing it."

"I'm not. Though I do feel like every time I turn around, I'm needing a nap."

"As long as you listen to your body and do it, you'll be fine. When do you go to the doctor again? I'd be happy to drive you."

Suddenly, Kandi flung herself at Anne, deep wrenching sobs exploding from her as her chest heaved.

"Kandi, honey. What's the matter?"

Kandi sat back and grabbed up a towel from nearby, using it to wipe her face. "I've been thinking a lot about—"

Everything clicked into place. "Your mom."

Sadly, Kandi's mother had abandoned her as a child, leaving her with her grandfather to raise. The pain and betrayal from her mother had crept back into her awareness.

Kandi grabbed Anne's hand. "You're my mom. And I love you. But yes, it makes me have doubts about being a mother. What if I'm not cut out to be a mom? What if I ever left..."

"None of that talk. Of course, you will be a good mother. Everyone has doubts and qualms about things. And just because someone failed you doesn't mean that you are going to repeat their mistakes. I've never been privileged to have a child, but I know deep in my heart that this child is going to be blessed by having you as their mother."

"Really?" Kandi sniffed.

"Really. I know it."

Kandi slumped down into a chair. "I should have, like, tried harder to make up with my mother before she died."

Anne patted Kandi on the back. "We all have regrets of what we could have done or said. There's no way that we'll get out of this life without at least one or two. We can only acknowledge our lives now and, if we can, clear the air. I mean, I can't believe that I thought Sorcha despised me. We let our pride and our unwillingness to share our feelings cause more problems than were needed. Now, you can't make amends with your mother, but you can go from here and live a great life. And be a wonderful mom. Okay?"

Kandi nodded and smiled at Anne before rising and giving her a hug. "I better do as much of this now as I can because it won't be long before hugging is going to get a lot harder. I'm already finding it hard to button my pants."

"I don't think that's baby. I think that's pizza." Anne winked.

"Did someone say pizza?" Carson opened the door, holding some boxes while Stewart followed behind, carrying another box and some bags.

"Oh shoot, we forgot to pick a movie before they got back."

"How about we change our plans and play a game instead?" Stewart asked.

"Okay, but I'm going to win." Anne answered back, her competitive spirit on full display.

CHAPTER FIFTEEN

Anne took the initiative the following week to discover if Miranda had any information about the basket she won and to find out if she was acquainted with Laurel.

Since it was a Monday, she knew that the newly opened apothecary wasn't open for business. With no way of getting in touch with Miranda, she figured she'd take a chance and drive up to her house. Even if Miranda wasn't at home, it would be a pleasant drive and Anne opened the windows, allowing the invigorating scent of the mountain air to permeate the car. The Rockies were always a sight to behold in the spring, with the snow that still clung to the mountaintops like a white blanket and the colorful wildflowers that bloomed wherever the sunlight touched the ground.

Taking the drive up to the house gave Anne the opportunity to ponder what would make an ideal gift for Kandi for the baby shower. Completing the last twist of the switchbacks, the house appeared, located on the border of the property. Whoever had positioned the house's design had obviously taken advantage of the spectacular views of the valley that could be seen from the back of the property. When Anne pulled up, she was met with loud music that was emanating from within the house.

Taking a few steps up to the front door, Anne pressed the doorbell, the sound of the chimes echoing through the house. While she waited, she glanced around to observe if she could locate any signs of a surveillance camera. As far as the eye could tell, the doorbell was just like any other, with no clues that anything was out of the ordinary. She also didn't spy anything nestled in the eaves. It was possible that Miranda hadn't updated her home with the most recent security technology. After a few moments had passed, she decided to ring the bell a second time.

No one came to the door.

After feeling increasingly frustrated, Anne

stopped and contemplated for a moment. She pondered to herself if the music was so loud that it would mask the ringing of the bell. Deciding on another tact, Anne beat on the front door with the large bronze knocker shaped like a deer's head.

Still no response.

Ugh, she must not be able to hear me. Not one to let that stop her, Anne took the sidewalk that led over to the four-car garage. Next to it, a gravel and flagstone path led to wooden steps up to a back deck.

She stopped and admired the view as the beautiful expanse of the valley appeared in front of her.

This is absolutely amazing. The view of the valley from the overlook is even more stunning than I'd expected it to be. It's no surprise that Miranda chose to remain here.

Anne made her way up the stairs, calling out a cheerful, yet loud, "Hello!" to announce her presence. "Anyone home?"

Noting the large bifold doors, she saw that they were open, allowing for the pleasant spring air to flow indoors. She yelled out again, "Hello? Miranda. It's Anne Freemont. Are you there?"

The music continued to play as Anne made her way across the expansive deck that ran the entire length of the home, wrapping around it at each end.

Her phone trilled just as she made her way to the open door. She grabbed her phone from the side pocket in her purse.

It was Hope.

She'd just said hello when she reached the open doors. She gasped as she looked inside.

Hope's voice came over the line. "Anne, it's Hope. I'm back. I want us to get together and chat."

"I'm at Miranda's right now."

Hope's voice took on a strange tone. "Oh? Well, okay. We can talk when you get back into town."

Anne inhaled deeply to soothe her frazzled nerves. Hope's words compelled Anne to pay attention. "Wait, you're back in town?"

"Yes, I got in last night. Why? Oh, also find

out if she got the basket she won. She'd rung Autumn to say that she never got it."

"I'm looking at a basket from your shop at Miranda's." She turned away from the tragic scene in front of her, making her way over to the deck railing. She needed to remain calm.

"Anne, is everything all right? You don't sound like yourself."

"I'm, well. No. I mean yes. I can see the basket was delivered. There's one here now."

"Well, glad it worked out."

"I wouldn't say that. Miranda is dead."

~~

Anne took a seat on the steps near the entrance, biding her time until the sheriff and the other people came. She was beyond relieved when a car drove around the corner, allowing her to rush over to him. "Carson!"

He refrained from embracing her. Most likely, he was asked to lend a hand with the call. "In order to avoid any potential problems, let's wait for Ruiz to arrive and then we can figure out what our plan should be."

"Plan? You mean, like I'm a suspect? Do I need a lawyer?" The words tumbled out.

"Anne. Take a breath. I'm not saying any of that. Do you want to sit in my car until he arrives? I think it may help you steady your nerves."

Anne nodded in agreement. "Okay."

Another vehicle arrived, and Undersheriff Ruiz stepped out of his car. Carson had wanted to resign completely, but this was a good transition until the next election cycle. Carson had promoted Ruiz to Undersheriff and had already expressed his recommendation that Ruiz take over for him when he retired.

"Carson. Anne." Ruiz touched his fingers to his hat in recognition. "What's the situation?"

Anne explained how she had tried ringing the bell on the front door, but the music was so loud she figured Miranda couldn't hear it. After trying a few times, she'd gone around back to find Miranda dead in the kitchen. In answer to Ruiz's question on entry, she responded that she hadn't entered the house, but called in the information in to dispatch right away. She had to give herself credit because she would have normally gone inside and done some snooping. However, this time she'd decided to stay out of it for once. She didn't know what had happened to Miranda, but one look was all it took to let Anne know that the woman was dead.

Whoever had wanted Miranda dead had finally succeeded. Anne was presented with a difficult decision to make. With Hope arriving home late last night, it seemed unlikely that she had somebody to provide an alibi for her. This marked the second time where Hope could be regarded as the primary suspect.

Anne was itching to be allowed to leave so she could go home to figure this out. First Laurel and now Miranda. There must have been some type of connection between the two of them. This caused Anne to ask herself if Laurel had been aiding Miranda in any of her plans. It was feasible that Laurel caused her own death by stealing the basket of mushrooms which had been intended for Miranda.

Both of them had come into conflict with

Hope at some point, which provided a commonality between the two. If others began to have the same thoughts, the last thing she wanted was for someone to put the blame on Hope. The only positive in the situation was that Hope had probably not informed anyone else about her return. Anne wanted to talk to Hope as soon as possible, so the less she intruded on now, the quicker they might let her leave.

She shoved her phone deep into her pocket, cognizant that she had not been completely honest about not engaging in some detective work since her phone contained a picture. She hadn't taken a picture of Miranda's dead body, but the bunch of items sitting on the counter where she'd pulled them from the basket. She needed Hope to look at them and see if anything looked out of place.

It seemed like it took forever for them to give her the go-ahead to leave. They would take her statement down at the station, so she didn't need to spend any more time there. She left Carson and got back into her car. Driving back down the mountain, she clung to the steering wheel, her mind blank as if it had received too much input and needed a break from thinking.

As Anne continued on to Hope's residence, it felt almost surreal to her, like the earlier events of the morning had been a figment of her imagination. She pulled into the back of the lot, parking her car close to a tree that shaded the parking lot.

Entering the backroom, Autumn was hard at work. "Oh, hi Anne. Did you get your basket?"

"Yes, thanks." She'd probably never hear the end of her throwing away the mushrooms she thought had come with it.

"You're welcome. I was going down the list of deliveries and saw that you were on the list to get one."

"Did you deliver out to Miranda's?"

"Yes, I did all the deliveries yesterday. Her's was the last one. Pretty late yesterday. Why?"

Anne didn't want to go into all the details with Autumn at this point. She'd let Hope tell her later.

"Just wondered."

She pointed toward the door to the stairs. "You can find Hope upstairs. She said to send you up when you arrived."

"Great." Anne took the stairs fairly quickly to the apartment that Hope had once shared with her mom, Faith, who was now in a memory care home.

Anne uttered a greeting as she pushed the door open slightly, entering the room. "Hope, it's me. Anne." She softly tapped the door and stepped into the living room, where Hope was lying down on the sofa, her journal and pen in her grasp.

Anne stopped in her tracks upon seeing Hope, something about the sight of her friend made her pause.

CHAPTER SIXTEEN

Despite the peculiar feeling she had, Anne made her way towards Hope. "Hey there. I am so grateful that you are back home with us. I've missed you."

With a slow movement, Hope stood up and placed the pen and journal she had been using on the table close to her. "I've missed you too. I apologize for having been so secretive about this. I shouldn't have acted the way I did. To tell you the truth, I wasn't thinking clearly, but that's no excuse for my behavior. I certainly should have answered your texts. I hope you'll forgive me."

Sitting in a chair next to the sofa, Anne spoke. "I feel like I should be asking you to forgive me. Hope, if I've upset you, please let me know. I wouldn't want anything to come between us. Our friendship means too much to me for that."

"There's no need for concern. You haven't done anything. I needed a brief break in order to clear my head, contemplate my options, and move forward. That's why I'm the one who should apologize. I didn't think it through or how my disappearing for a bit would affect others. But I knew that I couldn't think about the next steps if I stayed here."

"What are you talking about? You had to think about some next steps?"

Hope returned to the sofa and audibly sighed before continuing the conversation. "Yes, that's correct. This experience has given me the perfect opportunity to take a step back and think about the things I want in life."

Anne focused on Hope, feeling the familiar uneasiness creep back in. "I'm sorry, I feel lost here. I'm not sure what you are referring to, could you elaborate?"

She paused for a moment, her eyes cast downward towards her hands. "I had a health issue arise that's given me a bit of a scare. There's a possibility that I have...well, they think I may have breast cancer. Right now, they've given a preliminary diagnosis, but I have some more tests coming up."

"What?" Anne sat bolt upright in a sudden, reflexive motion. "Why didn't you tell me? What do we need to do? Oh, Hope, I'm so sorry."

"Anne, calm down. Your reaction is exactly why I needed to get away from all of this for a while and from helpful friends like you. I had to decide on my own. Just in case it turns out that I do have it."

"Oh, Hope. I feel absolutely horrible. I wish you would have said something." Anne felt the tumultuous emotions swelling inside her chest, yet she kept them in check.

"The fact is, I've spent all my time working. If I hadn't had enough education with my medical courses, I then decided to go off and pursue my herbalism degree. We're pretty much talking about a decade of constant college courses and working. And then, of course, now there's the Inn. Anne, I invited you here because I've come to a decision. Actually, a few decisions."

"Yes?" Anne was perched on the edge of the chair, anticipation building as she waited for Hope's next words.

"I've decided to put the Inn up for sale. I will purchase both your and Kandi's shares, but I must let it go. It's one more thing I don't need on my plate right now. I am going to take the necessary steps to close my practice."

"Are you positive that this is what you want to do, Hope? Your reputation has gained so much trust from many people."

"Well, they can trust someone else for a change. With the new people moving into town, I've already spoken with another doctor who plans on moving here, and I'm going to refer my patients to her."

Anne took in everything that Hope had said. "That seems like a lot of things to change in your life when you don't even know for sure if you have cancer. Aren't you putting the horse before the cart?"

Hope shook her head to signify her strong and unwavering convictions, making it clear she was adamant in her stance. "While this seems like it's a hasty decision, in reality, I've been feeling rather off and out of sorts for a significant period. My practice already causes a great amount of stress, and that's been compounded by the Inn and the Shoppe. My life revolves around working. Even when I'm not doing that, I'm either cleaning or ordering product, or so many other things that get pushed to the side."

She took a deep breath before resuming. "When have I had the time to focus on myself? As a person. It ultimately doesn't matter to me what the diagnosis is. Well, I take that back. Obviously, I hope it's good news, but no matter what, I've already come to terms with it. I've realized that I only have one life, it's become clear to me I've been working without living. Traveling is something that I would like to do, taking up painting or pottery as a creative outlet is a possibility, being a yoga teacher is something I'm interested in, but I'm not completely sure what I want to do. That's the thing. I have never really taken the opportunity to discover my identity or what I would like to become when I'm older. The phrase about a mid-life crisis is quite realistic. I never in my wildest dreams thought that this would be my fate. And yet, here we are." She gave a slight shrug of her shoulders.

Anne hadn't spoken as she recognized that much of what Hope shared was familiar. In her own life, Anne had picked up roots and moved to Carolan Springs after her divorce. She was all too familiar with the feeling that life was slipping away quickly, and she wanted to make the most of it. Like Hope, she'd been at a crossroads in her life, not knowing what she truly wanted, and decided to make the big move to Carolan Springs. But this was about Hope now, and she wanted to be the best friend she could. That meant simply listening and not giving any advice, which was difficult for Anne. She smiled at her friend. "Trust me, I do understand. I'm just happy to know that I didn't mess up somehow and make you mad at me. I'd hate to lose our friendship."

"No. I know that if I would've shared about what was going on, you would have wanted to jump in to give advice or to help. I needed to be alone to figure it out on my own."

Anne waited until Hope had finished

speaking before asking, "How soon can you expect to find out the diagnosis?"

"I'm going in for another ultrasound in a few weeks and I guess I'll find out after that if I'll have to go to the next test."

"I'm going with you. And don't give me any pushback. Whatever's coming, I want to be by your side."

"Anne, I so appreciate your friendship. Thank you."

" No, thanks needed. That's what friends do. Now, what about the Herbal Shoppe?"

"Autumn is going to take it over and I'll remain a silent partner. For now, I'm going to stay in this apartment until I've decided what I want to do and where I'll live. I don't plan on moving away, but at this juncture, I'm taking each day one step at a time. I figure I'll know what's going to happen by the end of the month. But either way, this allows me to take a step back."

"Hope, what can I do to support you?"

"Just be my friend. I've consulted with some specialists in case the news isn't good and I'm going to go off to do some alternative therapies that have proven successful in the past. Even if it's not cancer, it's my body giving me a wake-up call that I need to take care of myself. If it turns out to be true, then hopefully, I will have caught it early enough, so I don't have to have surgery. My goal is to keep it that way."

"How did you find out?"

"I'd been feeling off for some time. Tired, and noticed the lymph under my arm was swollen. I went and had a thermography. That's why I'm going in for an ultrasound. Of course, I've been given lots of recommendations on the best course of action from these physicians, but I have to do what I feel is best for me. If nothing else, I have control over what I'll try first."

"Such as?"

"There are a few places I'm looking into. One's in Sedona, there's a place in Mexico, and even one in India. I've been writing up all the pros and cons of each and think I'll head to Sedona first if the results aren't what I'd like. But right now, I'm thinking it's most likely other issues."

"A positive outlook is always a good thing." Anne said. "I think more important than just the treatments is that you surround yourself with people who love you."

"And that love you too."

"Oh Hope, I'm so sorry. I don't know what to say."

Hope made a tight mouth smile. "Just say you'll be my friend. Always."

"Always." Anne gulped back the threatening tears. "Of course, we are not going to give up hope that it isn't what they say it could be."

"Agree. Now, because I will be leaving for a while either way, I want to know about the plans you have for Kandi. She called and let me know that she's expecting."

"Yes, I said we could hold a baby shower for her. If you're going to be leaving soon, we should move it up so you can attend."

"That would be nice. I'm not sure how much the treatments will allow for me strength-wise, so that would be great if she wouldn't mind having it sooner than later." Hope sat up from the edge of the couch. "Oh, and Anne, I'm only telling you. I don't want anyone else to know. Not even Carson."

"Okay."

"Really?" Hope's eyes, shielded by her thick eyelashes, rose to meet Anne's gaze.

"You have my solemn promise." Anne crossed her heart as a sign of her solemn promise, then with great emphasis, acted out the locking of her lips with an imaginary key.

"Then that's all that matters. I trust you." She held out her hand and Anne grasped it in hers, for the first time noticing that the usually slim Hope had lost weight.

Hope sat back against the seat. "I'm so glad to get that off my chest, so to speak. Now, first things first. It sounds like we have another mystery to solve."

"First, I have a question for you. Kandi said that you had a fight with Laurel. Can you tell me what it was about?"

"I don't think it's worth talking about now that's she's gone."

Anne nodded, "I get it. But was it the fact that you found out she was stealing packages?"

Hope's face expressed her surprise. "Yes, how did you know about that?"

"Kandi and I went over to help clear out her house—that's another story—and found things she'd taken. Also, is it true that you told her something about her short, sad life?"

Hope sighed. "Yes. That was another thing that I had to think about. You know that my mother has what many have referred to as 'second sight'. It's not so much seeing anything, it's just a knowing. It's hard to describe. Well, it's passed down from mother to daughter. And as my mother is weakening, well, my awareness is growing. When I said what I did to Laurel, it stopped me in my tracks. Those words just came out of nowhere. But I knew they were true that she wouldn't have a long life. When I found out that she'd died, it was like a kick in the stomach. Words have power and I have to be more careful with things that just 'show-up' so to speak."

"I remember your mom saying some things,

but had no idea you had that gift too."

"Not sure it's a gift, but there are a lot of names for it. Second sight, prophecy, the list goes on. However, it often gets confused with being a psychic. I'm not and never will be."

"How is your mom?"

"Some days are better than others. Those are the days she recognizes me. But others, she's more withdrawn into herself."

Anne nodded, waiting for Hope to finish talking about her mom. Faith had been a mom to Hope during such a difficult time in her life, and Hope treasured their time together. They sat in silence for a minute until Hope glanced over at Anne.

"So, a new mystery. When do we get started?"

CHAPTER SEVENTEEN

Not wanting to change the subject, she realized that Hope needed a distraction after everything she'd just shared. Anne took a few moments to consider her response before giving her a reply. "Are you completely sure?"

Hope gave a small nod in agreement. "Taking my mind off this for a while and focusing on something else would be a great way for me to clear my head. So, let's start with this. Is it true that when you arrived at her house, you found Miranda dead?"

"Well, she had music blaring, so she didn't hear me ring the front doorbell. I went around back and that's when I found her."

"Got it. Were you able to tell what killed her?"

"I didn't go inside. There was no mistaking that she was dead, though. I could have gone inside as the door was one of those tri-fold doors like Sam has in his house, so open to the deck to let in the fresh air. So even though I wasn't 'in' the house, I was pretty close. There wasn't any apparent trauma, so for all I know, she could have had a heart attack or something like that. Oh, on another note, did I tell you I saw Sam at the garden shop?"

"He's back in town?"

"Yes. Sounds like he's tired of big city life, and said he missed the mountains."

"I can understand that. I don't know him all that well, as our paths don't really cross. I think I've seen him a few times, if that. One of those times was when you first moved here."

"Oh, yes. I remember that now. One of the very few times I've fainted in my life." Anne recalled the events that transpired when she'd first moved to Carolan Springs. It was funny to think about it now and how much time had passed since her arrival in the small Colorado mountain town.

"Now, back to Miranda."

"Hope, quick question for you. Sorcha said that you went to school with Miranda."

She scowled, but almost instantly changed

her facial expression to something more neutral. "Yes, why do you ask?"

"I don't know really, but I feel this all has something to do with things that happened years ago. I think poor Laurel may have just gotten caught up in it and that Miranda was the main target."

"Could be, I guess. The thing is, Miranda always felt the need to be better than others. I avoided her in school, but then she started picking on this new girl. I mean, it was constant. I once found her crying in the bathroom. That did it. I knew I'd regret it, but I confronted Miranda. As you can imagine, I became the hero of the hour with lots of other students who been on the receiving end of her vitriol. But I also had put a big target on my back."

"Hmm. Do you remember who she went after? That could be a clue."

"Let me think. Oh yeah, Cathy. Sweet kid. Yes, that's who it was. Cathy Landers."

Anne leaned toward Hope. "Wait a minute. Landers. That's Marcia's last name."

Hope nodded. "Yes, I believe that's when she and Marcia stopped being friends. Marcia was a senior, and her sister was a freshman. Miranda was a junior. Marcia didn't know how Miranda treated others until she found out what she'd done to her sister." Hope stood from where she was sitting and walked over to the small kitchen area and opened the fridge. "Want some sparkling water with some grapefruit juice?"

"That sounds great. Sure." Anne watched as Hope poured freshly squeezed grapefruit juice into tall tumblers, then added the sparkling water on top.

She handed the glass to Anne. "Here you go."

"Um, yummy. Hits the spot." Anne moved a coaster over on the table and set down her drink. "It sounds like she was something back when she was a teenager."

"Well, her parents had money, and that went to her head. She treated others as beneath her."

"Even you?"

"Oh, you don't know all the fun that people have at your expense when they call your mom the town witch. Miranda was always at her core, a bully. She would do everything in her power to cause disruption but then sit back and laugh as others went at each other. I didn't even know she was back until someone told me. Who was it? Oh, yes. I'm pretty sure it was Laurel."

"Is that what you were fighting about?"

Hope shook her head. "No. Like you said earlier, I'd caught her trying to take a package off the back porch. I told her if she didn't stop it, I'd have no choice but to report her. She told me to try it and see what happened. That my shop would be closing down soon enough. I'd tried to be nice, but I was already dealing with my own issues, and I was tired—"

"Hope, you don't have to explain yourself to me. Look at the mess I was in when I moved here, and my hormones were all over the place."

"Oh boy, do I remember that!" She smirked.

"Ha. Ha. Funny. I wasn't that bad."

In response to Anne's statement, Hope contorted her face into a funny expression.

"Okay, maybe I was. But I didn't know that

my hormones would cause such havoc with my emotions and moods. But thanks to you, and mother nature, that's all past me now."

"And a good thing, too." Hope laughed.

"Okay, so if Miranda caused so much trouble when she was young, doesn't it seem weird that she'd want to move back here?"

"You know what they say about time and memories. Plus, she's got—let me rephrase that, had that beautiful house her parents left her. Much better to come back here and be a big fish in a small pond than to a small fish in a big pond. I just hope she's grown up since those days, though."

Anne yelled out. "Ha! You just proved your innocence."

Hope shook her head. "Whatever are you talking about? Sometimes—"

"You just talked about her as if she's still alive. You said, 'I hope she's grown up'. Versus something in past tense."

"Sometimes I really wonder how your mind works. I often think you and Kandi have more in common than either of you admit."

Anne didn't respond to Hope's statement, continuing with their conversation thread. "So besides calling you out because of your mom, did anything else happen for her to still resent you?"

"Well, of course, I was dating the boy she wanted."

"What? Spill." Anne downed some more of her grapefruit drink as Hope took a big sip of her juice drink.

"Yes, he'd received acceptance to the CIA. When he chose me to take to the homecoming dance, she was absolutely furious. Unexpected events started occurring, such as someone keying his car and suspicious brown bags filled with you-know-what being left on our doorstep. There were even more nasty rumors circulating around the school and the local community. Some pretty malevolent. Of course, it devastated me, but my mother didn't seem fazed by it all. No one knew exactly how Miranda always got the gossip started, but she had a special knack for it. Here and there, a misplaced word, a jumbled phrase, or even a whole sentence spoken where others could overhear and then it was off growing by itself. Then, out of the blue, my date to the dance failed to show up and provided no explanation. Of course, as a young girl, I was crushed, but I refused to go to the dance alone and let Miranda rub it in. From that point on, I never laid eyes on him again. And it wasn't too long after that, she must have gone a step further. Her father fired his dad from his company, and his family moved not long afterwards."

"Geez. She really was a piece of work" Anne thought even more that Miranda starting her business wasn't one more thing to get back at Hope. Even though she'd heard all the gossip and known that sales were down, she didn't want to share that with her. She needed encouragement, not discouragement at what Miranda had pulled.

Hope took a sip of the cool drink. "You could say that."

"Oh, I forgot. I took a picture of the counter where your basket was sitting. Anything look out of place?" She showed the picture to Hope, who scanned the bottles, soaps, and other items on the counter.

"Hold on. Can you make the picture bigger?"

Anne used her fingers to enhance the frame as Hope stared at the picture. Her mouth gaped open when she turned to Anne.

"Anne, we need to call Carson right away. I think I may know what killed Miranda."

Anne glanced back at the picture. "What? Did I miss something?"

Hope replied. "This." She pointed to a tincture of Hope's that showed it had been opened, the seal unwrapped.

Anne read the label on the front of the bottle. "Osha tincture. I don't understand. What am I missing?"

"That was the box that had been taken. I had made some for a client who lives over by the Montrose area. But look at the bottle. It's my bottle, but that's not the seal I use. Someone tampered with the bottle. If I had to guess, they dumped the real osha tincture and replaced it with a deadly version. Probably hemlock, which is extremely poisonous."

"What do you mean? The Shakespeare stuff?"

"Not exactly. Hemlock is another plant that is often mistaken for osha root. But it's deadly to animals, and of course, humans. Two to three bites will kill you. Now imagine it in a concentrated tincture. Only certified or skilled herbalists should work with collecting osha root, not unlike someone that works with mushrooms. You have to know that it's the right root. That's why most herbalists won't even divulge the aspen grove where they've found the osha root. Whoever did this must have had the knowledge to identify the plant, harvest it safely, and then create a tincture with it. "

"That means it was premeditated murder. If Laurel had taken the mushrooms meant for Miranda, they had to come up with another plan." Plan. There was that word again. "Hold on! I just remembered something." Anne browsed through her phone. "I came across a broken bottle in the alleyway. I wonder if the bottle broke, and they threw it out of the vehicle?" She showed Hope the picture.

"Yes, and look at the label. This is the formula for the osha tincture that we have created." Hope's face was filled with dismay as she leaned back against the sofa. "Someone's trying to make it seem like I'm the one who caused Miranda's death."

"And possibly, Laurel's too."

"But who and why go to all this trouble?"

"Who knows? But you'll be glad to know that I saved that bottle. Unless they wore gloves, their fingerprints will be on the bottle. We can give it over to the police and let them know."

A thought came to Anne. "Hope, do you know Marcia? She runs the mushroom group."

"Oh yes. Like I said, she was one of Miranda's best friends in high school until she found out she'd been bullying her baby sister. Then they had a falling out. I think it was over a boy, too. I guess Marcia finally got a look at the real Miranda, and what she'd do to get her way."

"The question is, how badly did Marcia resent her, and if she's now seeking her revenge after

Miranda moved back?" Anne thought back to the note in Laurel's book about M and the plan. It was certainly possible that Marcia was the M that Laurel referred to in her journal.

"Hope, you didn't also have a falling out with Marcia, did you?"

"Yes, but that was ages ago. It's all water under the bridge now."

Anne's gaze met Hope's at the same moment. If it were true that revenge was a dish best served cold, had Marcia waited to take hers on both of her old school classmates?

CHAPTER EIGHTEEN

Even with Anne's desire to dig deeper into what happened to Laurel and Miranda, most of her days and nights were spent worrying about Hope and preparing for Kandi's baby shower. She'd gotten the go-ahead with the French Bistro to reserve the patio area for the event, which would start at one in the afternoon. After the breakfast crowd was done, they'd have the place to set up the decorations and for the staff to prepare the buffet for the guests.

As Anne carefully placed the basket filled with party favors that the guests would be taking with them when they left, Hope came over to see what was happening.

"Anne! You look wonderful. I love that green on you." Hope came to her and enveloped her in a comforting hug.

"Hello to you too. You're in a good mood." She added a few more presents to the basket to make it more complete.

"I should be. I have been medically cleared. No cancer. They want me to come back in six months just to re-check, but it's only dense tissue with a bit of inflammation. Turns out my new bras were pinching my shoulder and I'd also picked up a bad habit of leaning on my left arm when I was on the computer, so that didn't help with the lymph." Hope broke down crying. "I was so scared. I thought—"

"Please don't cry. You'll get me started too, and this is the first time I've worn mascara in forever." Tears ran down her face as she let out a chuckle that soon turned into a fit of laughter. "Too late. Hope, this is a miracle, our prayers have been answered. I'm so happy." Wrapping her in another hug, she stepped away from her and then searched in her purse for a tissue. She wiped under her eyes, hoping that she wouldn't end up looking like a raccoon. "Phew, I'm relieved that is done! I'm glad that you took the time to tell me about this. By doing that, today's celebration will be even more special."

Thankfully, they had a few moments to

themselves before a few wait staff appeared and assisted Anne with moving some tables around. "Thanks. This will be helpful to have the buffet served from both sides." Even though the group was smaller, this would also free up the space.

Soon, Kandi arrived, dressed in a pretty pink and white outfit. She surveyed the scene with its baby items on display. "I can't believe this. I'm going to be a mother. How wild is that!"

"Pretty wild. But I know that you'll be excellent at it. Just like you are at everything else." Anne said.

"Ah, thanks, Mom." Kandi responded before she went to the end of the table to look at the cake that had been set up. She glanced over Anne's outfit. "That combination of the emerald dress and yellow sweater looks gorgeous on you. Is it new?"

"Yes. I went to Cherry Creek and found it." Anne had debated on the darker shade of green than the traditional colors of springtime, but it would still be a great transition option to wear when paired with a variety of jackets or sweaters.

She carefully brushed her hands down the front of her clothing, making sure there wasn't any lint on it. She left Kandi admiring the party favors as she moved around, checking tables and name tags.

Anne looked around, trying to remember everything on her list that she had to do. The guests arrived and everyone enjoyed cranberry or orange mimosas or sparkling cider. After everyone had taken their seats, they had groups go up and help themselves to the buffet that comprised wonderful quiches, an assortment of spring salads, and crystal goblets of strawberries Romanoff. Conversation flowed easily between the tables as everyone enjoyed the delicious food prepared by the Bistro.

Hope leaned close to Anne, lowering her voice to a whisper. "Anne, this is absolutely wonderful. You've done a great job. Kandi will certainly cherish this day as the perfect dream come true."

"Thanks. This is what's important. Not snooping into things that I don't know how to solve. This is when we need your old friend from the CIA." She gave a hearty laugh.

"CIA? How's that?"

"You know, you said your old friend from school got accepted into the CIA."

Hope's brows knit together before she responded with a chuckle. "Oh, sorry. Not that CIA. Culinary Institute of America."

"Oh, okay. I misunderstood" A flash of movement behind a screen set up for taking out used dishes caught her attention. But she spun back to the group as one of Kandi's friend's stood and shared about her long-time friendship with Kandi.

Listening to the woman, Anne abruptly remembered that she had left Kandi's present in her SUV that was parked out back. She was unsure of the timeline for when gifts would be opened, but she wanted to be present before the cake was cut and served. "Hope, I left Kandi's gift in my car. I'll be back in a jiff." Retrieving her keys from her purse, she moved toward her car through the back entrance.

As the back door opened, someone yelled out, "Mike, can you tell us where you'd like these boxes of mushrooms stacked?"

As if a set of tumblers had engaged in her mind, they clicked over and over.

Mike.

Mushrooms.

Laurel wouldn't have given a thought to mushrooms he'd given her. That meant she hadn't taken items from Miranda's. A shiver went up her spine as she slowly turned around. It was the good-looking waiter from the day she and Kandi had dined there.

Their eyes met.

The look on his face confirmed that he knew she'd figured it out. Striding over to her, he grabbed her arm, twisting it hard, before she could make it back into the event.

He gripped her arm even tighter. "I would hate for Kandi to have a horrible case of food poisoning that lands her in the hospital."

Anne gasped. "Please, no. Don't hurt them."

"Then you won't do something stupid like scream or make a fuss. Here's what's going to happen. We're going for a ride. You go get in your car and pull up to the curb. I'll get in there. Where's your phone?"

"In my purse. On the back of the chair."

"Good. Making any wrong moves and I will forward this note to a different waiter." He presented her with a photo of a solitary piece of cake that had the word Mama intricately spelled out on top.

The text read: Had to leave. Give to special guest.

Anne's heart was pounding in her chest as her body was consumed with fear. "How do I know you won't do that, anyway?"

"You don't. Now move."

Anne's hands shook as she struggled against bolting. But where could she go? Could she make it back into Kandi before he caught up with her and Kandi was served the cake or something else? She had no way to call her or Hope, and if he sent that text, would she have time to stop Kandi from partaking? Anne knew that she had to create some time. She got in the vehicle, thinking about how she could signal someone without him seeing. A knock on the glass caused her to jump. She unlocked the passenger door, and he got in the vehicle with her.

He twisted to face her. "Now drive."

"You're not going to get away with this. They're going to wonder where I am right now."

"I don't think so." He replied calmly.

"Why do you say that?"

"Because I took your purse and your phone when they were all watching your young friend head over to the gifts for a picture. I told one guest that you'd forgotten the present at home and would be back shortly to go ahead with opening presents." He held up her phone while he ditched her purse in the backseat.

"Well, that's not going to take long. They're going to realize that I've been gone too long."

He made a sad face, his mouth in a pout. "Sadly, this town is becoming more populated and so many bad people moving in, it was a matter of time before there was a carjacking. Kids, these days."

Anne drove on, wondering if she should go

slower or speed up and get someone's attention that way. However, he held his phone, and she couldn't take the chance that he would text the waiter. "No one's going to believe that. And I'm sure that someone had to have seen you with me. I mean, you'd be missed too."

"I don't really care what they believe. Sadly, you've gotten so involved in this last case that you were never seen again. And my shift was over. For all they know, I won't be back until dinnertime. At which time, I'll be long gone out of the country."

Anne gulped. One of the first rules of being kidnapped was to never, ever leave the scene. That your chances were best at the beginning. But what if it had meant he'd harm Kandi or the baby? Think. Think. She had to figure a way out of this. "Where are we going?"

"To Miranda's."

"Mirandas?"

"Yes, it seems appropriate. Actually, her parents' home. It's a bit like a full circle."

Anne thought to herself quickly and inquired, "Were you acquainted with her parents?"

His laughter had a dark and menacing undertone. "She destroyed my family, and I got to destroy hers."

"What do you mean?"

His jaw clenched. "Miranda couldn't stand it when I rejected her in high school. She thought I would be grateful to even be in her presence. She always thought that everything revolved around her. After I rejected her advances, she went and told her father that I'd tried to get too friendly, if you get my drift. Her father broached the topic with my dad. My father made the blunder of defending me by saying that she was not being truthful about what had happened. My family was already having difficulty making ends meet, and the firing of my father put us in an even worse financial situation. It was necessary for them to declare bankruptcy, and as a result, my father began to drink heavily. I'd had a scholarship, but that was mysteriously withdrawn 'after careful consideration' of the board. Her destructive behavior ruined my life and the life of my family in more ways than one."

"So, everything fell into place when Miranda's dad died?" Anne attempted to relax her hold on the steering wheel in order to reduce the stress in her muscles and body.

"Oh, it fell into place alright. I needed to get Miranda to come back here for my plan to work. I was going to just cause her some problems, but I changed my mind. An eye for an eye, and all that. The sadness and anguish endured by my father in his life took its toll and led to his untimely death and burial in an early grave. Why shouldn't I do the same to hers? Individuals who have a considerable amount of money often have an interesting perspective on things, for instance... they never even glance at the wait staff. Her mother had already left the old man, but he had a dinner party, and I was their chef. Let's just say that I left him a meal that I knew he would absolutely die for." The sound of his laughter sent chills down her spine.

Anne was overwhelmed with a barrage of thoughts, her mind racing to keep up. He'd killed Miranda's father to get her to come home. This man was a psychopath or sociopath. She never could keep her 'paths' straight other than to know that she wouldn't be able to speak to his humanity. There was none in him.

Her hands gripped the steering wheel as she drove, trying to listen but also think of what she could do to escape. He continued.

"You know it's funny. I almost let her live. She decided to stay here and well, 'as the spider said to the fly,' why not have a bit of fun, first? I thought of getting revenge on all the girls who'd rejected me in school."

"You mean like Hope? She didn't. Miranda made that up."

His growl was intimidating enough to make her distance herself from him. "Don't try to fool me. I know she did."

"But she didn't. I'm telling you the truth. What good would it do me to tell you differently?" Their closeness was so discomforting. If only she could move away from him.

"None. But that wouldn't stop you from trying." He attempted to smile at her, yet his eyes remained cold and unresponsive. It felt as if the person who had waited on them had just been acting out a role, and now the real monster had been revealed.

Anne forced her voice to remain calm, even though she was frantic with fear. "I'm telling you the truth."

He swiveled in his seat. "That is unfortunate. Although it is rare, friendly fire can occur."

"Listen, you don't have to do this."

He threw back his head and laughed. "Oh, my gosh. It's like you've read too many mysteries. This isn't a TV show. You can't talk your way out of this."

"I'm not trying to do that. Okay, to be honest, maybe I am. Just saying that you don't have to do this. I mean, maybe Miranda's death could be contributed to an accident. You could get off."

"Miranda. Ah, Miranda. You know that she didn't even recognize me. Of course, why would she? I was a lanky and awkward looking teenager with spots, glasses, and a prominent overbite the last time she saw me. It's amazing what braces, contacts, a nose job, and lifting weights along with growing five inches does to you. No one else recognized me either. Though Marcia asked if we'd met before. That threw me. I almost had to add her to my list."

A list. Did murderers have a to do list for killing?

And why would anyone recognize him if he'd had that much work done? Anne had to admit that with his designer haircut, straight white teeth, piercing stormy blue eyes, and strong physique, he was handsome in a serial killer kind of way. She almost broke out into manic laughter. The fear was taking hold, and she had to hold her wits about her if she was going to survive this. It wouldn't be long before they'd be at the turnout for the road to Miranda's.

Think.

Think.

There was no way she could fight back against him. She had to get away from him. If nothing else, she had to make sure that he wouldn't hurt anyone else. The next words echoed in her mind.

Or die trying.

CHAPTER NINETEEN

Anne slowed the car to a stop, her hand on the door in case she needed to jump out.

"Now, here's what's going to happen. You're going to drive up around the garage. Back there is a dirt track. Take it until I tell you to stop."

As Anne drove her vehicle slowly down the lane between the trees, she could hear the branches scratching against the metal. The car made its way through the tall grass, its front bumper lightly tapped by the blades as it drove. Although the road had previously been kept up, the forest had gradually taken it back, making the journey slow and difficult for them.

"It looks like we need to exit the car and journey the rest of the way on foot. At least it's a nice day for it. Don't you think?"

Anne remained quiet and said nothing. The man was certifiably crazy. As he opened the car door, the sound of a tree branch scraping the paint created a sound similar to the sound of chalk being dragged across a chalkboard. Anne cringed at it, shaking off the chill that went up her spine.

Should she remain in the car or risk getting out? By going outside, she thought she might have a better chance. In the car, he would quickly overpower her. Anne hesitated before opening the door. Maybe she could put the car in reverse. As if he could read her thoughts, he said, "I'll take those keys."

She glanced down at the set and, picking it up, decided that she had to at least slow him down. She pushed open the door and practically fell out of the vehicle. Pulling her arm back, she launched the keys into the air. Unfortunately, her throwing arm left much to be desired, and they landed in a puff of dirt, not far from the back of the car. So much for hindering him.

He looked on as the keys flew a few yards away from the back of the automobile. With an expression of disbelief, he shook his head and raised his eyebrows in surprise. "Really?"

"You can't fault me for trying."

He grinned, and it was at that moment she knew that he was toying with her. She needed to keep him talking. Maybe that would give her some time before he made any move toward her. "What about Laurel?"

He laughed again. "Don't you think I know your ruse to keep me talking? But I have time. So why not? I'll play along. Ah, that kid. Seemed nice enough. The problem was she stole from me. I don't like it when people steal from me. But like many young women, she was gullible. All I had to do was let her know I forgave her and act like we had so much in common. As soon as she shared about some bullies back home, I knew I'd found someone who could help me achieve my plan. Now, of course, she didn't know that my plan involved murder. She thought it was a bit of revenge, nothing harmful. But then she made the mistake of starting to ask questions. She'd been feeding me information about Hope and Miranda. I was going to have one take the blame for the other one's death. I realized Laurel was a loose thread. So, she had to go. It was simple to supply her with the extra mushrooms I'd had from the restaurant. Of course, I added a few other not so delightful ones to the mix. Even better, she'd taken Miranda's basket that she'd won at the presentation. I couldn't have planned it better myself."

"And Miranda? Did you have Laurel take the bottles from Hope's?"

"Actually, no. But when I found that Laurel had taken them, it was just a matter of time before I came up with an idea that would connect the two."

"We didn't see the bottles when we went to Laurel's house."

"Oh, you wouldn't have. They were in the back of her car. She used to do some dishwashing for the restaurant when it first opened."

So that was how their paths had crossed. Anne wondered how long he'd put up with her attempt to keep him talking before he attacked. She had to try. "But how did you get the tincture into Miranda's basket?"

"Oh, that worked out perfectly. Autumn came

in to grab some bread and I heard her say she was making deliveries. I simply went out to her car and saw that she had one for Miranda. She'd left the doors open, so it was easy to add in the tincture I'd already prepared. That actually worked out better than my original plan. I just love serendipity." He stopped talking and his voice took on a menacing tone.

"Now, we can't stand on either side of this vehicle all day."

"I don't know. Works for me."

"You're funny. I like that. But both of us know that I'm bigger, stronger, and faster than you. You're just putting off the inevitable. Walk!" He pointed down the path which led deeper into the forest, with foliage growing dense along the sides.

Anne set off down the path, leaving a space between her and Mike. As the forest grew denser, the path grew smaller, not unlike a deer trail or other hiking path. She slowed as she stumbled over a large tree root, and he caught up to her, pushing her toward a nearby tree. She caught herself before she fell to the ground. Anne's entire body was on full alert, but she realized that Mike was drawing this out, enjoying every moment. If nothing else, it gave her time to think. And with that time, realization took hold.

"How do I know that you won't hurt Kandi or Hope?"

"I said it before. You don't."

She made a mad dash towards the tree branch in front of her, quickly grabbing it and yanking it forward with all her might, praying that it would not snap. "Then I can't let that happen." She pushed the branch away with considerable force and speed, ducking under it as it flew backward.

It slapped Mike in the face, causing him to scream out in pain. Anne knew she had seconds before he would recover and come after her. With relief, she stumbled down the path, grateful that she had worn flats instead of the high heels she had thought about wearing to Kandi's shower.

Her heart was pounding as she realized that he would soon be back on his feet and coming after her, so she hastened down the path. She raced to the big log that had been toppled across the path and scurried underneath it. As she moved forward, she noticed that there were large clusters of boulders located both to her left and right. If she chose the uphill route, she knew it would be more strenuous and he would probably assume she had taken the easy way out and gone down the hill. As she glanced around, she spotted a considerable sized rock and chucked it down the hill, which caused the loose stones to slip and slide.

Looking behind her, along the path she had taken, she still didn't spot any sign of him. He could still be fighting with the pine needles that that had fallen on him and attempting to remove the sticky sap from his face and hands. There would be no delays now that she'd fought back and injured him. Although it would give her more time, it also meant that his anger would be increasing in its intensity with every passing moment. That wouldn't be good for her. To deceive him, she had to make him believe that she had gone down the hill to create distance between them. She pulled off her yellow cardigan and wadding it up, flung it down the hill. This time, a breeze caught it so that it landed further than the bad attempt with the keys. She whispered a thank you before turning back the way she'd come. Hopefully, it would cause him to head in that direction in order to give her a chance to get up the hill on the other side. For now, she moved back toward the large log and, making her way to a gully, pushed herself into a muddy bank, pressing leaves in around her and trying to camouflage herself as much as possible.

She only hoped that he'd spot the bright color in the distance and not look too hard around the log. She lowered her head and waited. It wasn't long before she heard him moving toward her.

This could be it. She held her breath, ready to fight if necessary.

Thankfully, she heard him grunting as he climbed over the log. Unlike her, he couldn't fit underneath, which also meant that he might not spot where she'd concealed herself.

She stifled a scream as his voice, close to her hiding place, called out. "You can't hide from me.

I know these woods like the back of my hand."

Anne bit her lip, holding her breath as he moved down the path. Was he tricking her? She couldn't be sure, but she had to make a move for it. She lifted her head to see that he was looking down the hill from the path and up the other side, figuring out his options.

Choosing at last, he disappeared behind the rock face as Anne bolted from her spot. Staying close to the ground and behind the large log, she struggled up the hill face, stopping every few moments to listen. The only thing she heard was the wind blowing through the trees.

Once she made it to where the boulders were larger, she pulled herself up to the top. Already she could tell the sun would be sinking in the west, making it dark in the mountains, where other dangers lurked. She took a breath and leaned up against the rock face. As she did so, she spied a small opening in the bottom. Could she squeeze in there? If she did, and he found her, she'd be trapped. But she had to take that chance.

Feeling helpless, she made her way to the

cramped space. She drew her legs close, wrapping her dress around her tightly as her entire body trembled, surrendering to the jumble of emotions inside her.

I'm going to die out here.

No one will ever know what happened to me.

Her hands and knees, now bruised and burning from her grabbing the branch and her struggle up the hill, kept her mind alert. Every sound seemed magnified. As she bent her head to her knees, a thought came to her. He hides me in the cleft of the rock. Her faith had always been there, but now it seemed more real than ever before.

It felt like time stood still and each minute and second felt like an eternity. How long would it take him to discover where she was located? If she decided to stay here, how much time would pass before the cold of the night induced hypothermia? Thankfully, the dress had three quarter length sleeves.

Even if he left, as soon as the darkness of night descended upon the land, the animals that roamed the area became powerful predators. Without the light to guide her, it was entirely possible that she could become lost and lose the path. She wouldn't be able to leave even if he left her there. Instead of the fear, peace passed over her. It was doubtful that there was cell service out here, so he couldn't call the restaurant. Plus, by now, they had probably finished the shower. If nothing else, she had ensured that nothing would happen to those she loved. He couldn't go back into town in her car, so that meant he'd have to leave town. If it meant that she lost her life, saving those of Kandi and her unborn child and Hope's were worth it.

Every ounce of energy had been used up, and her hands and legs were shaking from exhaustion. She was concerned that the adrenaline rush would soon wear off, leaving her powerless to fight back. She rested her head against the hard surface of the rock. Even though it was cool to the touch, its strong support comforted her. Unexpectedly, she felt her eyelids grow heavy and her body giving into the need of rest.

She was dreaming.

Carson called for her. "Anne, Anne, where are you?"

She wanted to reach him, but she couldn't. Her hands kept hitting rock. Anne bolted awake. Someone was calling her.

But what if it was Mike?

Other voices joined in. Hope's. Sam's.

She yelled out, "I'm here! I'm in here." She tried to stand, but her legs wouldn't hold her. She heard the crunching of boots and the next thing, strong, warm hands were pulling her from her shelter.

Carson embraced her. "Oh, Anne. Please don't ever do that to me again."

"I won't." She whispered.

"Promise."

"I promise. What happened to...is Kandi alright? How did you find me?"

Sam came over and slipped a heavy, warm blanket over her shoulders. He interjected. "All that later. First, we need to check you out. Do we need to get the stretcher?"

"No, I think I can walk." She stumbled. "Maybe."

"Okay, let's have a lot at your vitals first." After his evaluation, he said, "You may be a bit dehydrated, but I don't see anything that looks threatening. Any aches or pains anywhere?"

"No. Just my hands and my legs." She looked down at her dress, releasing that the dark color she'd chosen had most likely helped to save her life. Carson's strong arms and the heavy blanket anchored her, and she felt some of her strength returning.

She heard Sam say, "Sip this electrolyte drink for me. Once we get back to the house, we can look at the cuts on your hands and legs. Anything else I can do for you right now?"

"I don't suppose you brought some popcorn with you?"

They broke out laughing as Carson stared at the two of them.

CHAPTER TWENTY

Anne moved gingerly as she made her way out of bed. Even with daily warm Epsom salt baths and staying in bed, her body was letting her know of her escapades through the dense forest. After a few days of being back home, Carson finally reprimanded her for disregarding his warnings and leaving with Mike. Knowing that Anne had been in precarious events before, he had thought ahead and placed a tracking device on her car shortly after they had married. His forward thinking had been a relief to him and deliverance for her.

One a cop, always a cop.

At any other time, Anne may have been angry at him for adding the device to her car. But one fact remained. It had probably saved her life. That and Hope calling him as soon as she hadn't returned to the shower. Hope knew it wasn't like Anne to leave like that. She wouldn't have left without a word to anyone. And then she'd received a strange text that didn't sound like Anne at all. When she'd replied, there had been no response. That's when Hope knew something had happened. Plus, she could have given Kandi the present at home. Anne was thankful that both had known her so well.

She made her way into the bathroom, where she surveyed her face. After arriving home, she'd ended up spending a couple of days in bed from the stress and exhaustion of the experience. When she'd wake up, she'd found Carson next to her or snoozing in a chair he'd pulled up next to the bed. She didn't know what she'd done to deserve such a loving man, but she was thankful. She was also grateful that they'd apprehended Mike, who would spend the rest of his days behind bars. Anne doubted that the people he'd killed in Carolan Springs were his only victims and other crimes were being looked into as well.

But that didn't matter now. What mattered was being with her family and friends. Like Hope had experienced, this had been a wake-up call for Anne. To be more present with those she loved, to take stock of her life and what she wanted, and to not waste another precious minute on senseless actions or ideas. She went out into the garden, letting the sun hit her face. Pulling the trowel from the garden container, she plunged the spade into the earth. Moaning as the soreness in her knees and legs made itself known, she stopped and repositioned herself. While the pain wasn't great, it was a reminder that she needed to spend more time in that position—on her knees, humbling herself and being reminded of how blessed she was.

Making her way down the stairs, she went to the enclosed porch where she'd set her spring bulbs and other plants. She opened a bag of dahlia roots—dark and dirty, nothing like the beauty that they would become that summer. This garden bed would spring forth with glorious color, just as her life had grown. Today, she would relish the moment and be grateful for everything.

~~

The sound of children's laughter and squeals of joy echoed through the cul-de-sac as they played. As Hope had stated, she'd put the Brandywine Inn up for sale and a large family had moved into the house next door. After remarrying, this couple had a unique family dynamic, with teenagers and toddlers living together under the same roof. The wife was also pregnant, expecting a new addition to the family. She gave a wave in the direction to where Kandi had appeared; her growing pregnancy causing her to radiate with a healthy glow. As Anne looked on, she saw the two of them chatting in the area where their yards joined. They looked over at her and she waved to them in greeting. She let out an audible sigh, her breath heavy with emotion. The once sleepy cul-de-sac had become a bustling community because of the influx of new neighbors with children.

Hearing the door open, she looked over her shoulder to see Carson emerging from inside. In his hand, he held two cups and moved to sit with her on the porch swing. "It occurred to me you might be interested in having a cup of coffee."

"Thanks. I'll probably regret it later when I

can't sleep, but it sounds wonderful." She gratefully accepted the mug he offered her.

Sitting on the porch swing, he tenderly draped his arm around her shoulders. "It's nice to see so many children outside playing."

"It is. I love it. Kandi has now gained not just new neighbors but also a network of people nearby who can help, plus she now has the benefit of having potential babysitters should the need arise."

Carson sipped at his coffee, remaining silent.

"Carson—"

"Yes?"

"Let's move out to your place. Sam's found a place and I think I'd like a break. We could rent this place out first before we decide about living there full time."

"Really? I thought you loved it here." He slowly drew away, gazing deeply into her eyes as he took in her features.

"I do. But I also know you miss being out in the forest. I have been living in this large house for a while now and I think I am finally at the point where I can take a break from it. Your house would make it easier to manage and would make it much simpler for us to travel. Now that you are retiring, I know you can take your writing to wherever you want to go, and I've been wanting to explore some new places. What do you say?"

"I say that sounds great." With tenderness, he placed a kiss on her forehead. "You don't think you'll miss being so close to Kandi?"

"I've given it a lot of thought. I will do what I can to help, but there are other mothers who will be there to provide her with the support she needs. I've never had children and—"

"Despite that, it doesn't mean you haven't performed the role of a mother. The way you have been a great mom to Kandi is inspiring, and you will be an incredible grandmother when that time comes. I don't want you doubting yourself." He took her hand in his own.

"Thanks. I know. I have this overwhelming feeling that I need to do something. I can't describe it, really."

"You don't have to justify your actions to me.

It's fine. If it's your wish to move in order to be happy, then we will strive to make that dream come true. On another note, any word from Hope?"

"Just a few texts. She's taking some time with Faith and then doing a bit of travel for health. Even though she believes the danger has passed, she wants to make sure that nothing like this ever happens again. I think that when it's all said and done, she'll probably stay in Carolan Springs. But who knows?"

The sound of meowing came to them. They turned to see Minnie and Mouser sitting by the open window.

"And what about Minnie? Are you going to save the cat?"

"Well, Mouser has fallen for her, so I don't feel it's fair to him to make her leave now."

"Um, sure." He hid his grin with his coffee cup. "Anne—"

"Yes?"

"Thanks for moving to Carolan Springs and falling in love with this old man."

"I should be the one saying thank you. For putting up with my sticking my nose into everything, for rescuing me, but most importantly, for loving me, just as I am."

He moved his arm and gathered her hand in his big, beefy one. Kissing it lightly, he sighed. "Aren't we the lucky ones?"

~~

Thanks for reading Fungi Foul Play. I hope you enjoyed it and if so, please leave a review on your favorite retailer or reader site. I can often be found writing new stories about the residents of Carolan Springs as well as other characters. If you'd like to know more about them, you can sign up for my newsletter to stay up to date on upcoming releases, sales and freebies of similar authors, and fun contests and giveaways. In addition to signing up for my newsletter, you'll receive a fun short cozy mystery with all my characters that isn't available on any retailer.

When four amateur sleuths get together, mayhem and murder are sure to follow!

Seeking time away from daily life, Anne, Hope, Christie, and Viviane all find themselves at a spa together. But their idea of a relaxing time of pampering is ruined when another guest is killed, and Callie, a young staff member, is accused of being involved when jewelry goes missing. Working as a team, the sleuths work to clear Callie's name and track down a killer before they strike again.

Included are four yummy smoothie recipes— perfect for spring and summer!

This short read combines four sleuths into one light-hearted cozy, perfect for reading on an airplane, waiting for an appointment, or lounging by a pool. The story includes three different cozy mystery series characters: Anne and Hope from the Backyard Farming Mystery Series, Christie from the Taylor Texas Mystery Series, and Viviane from Viviane's Adventures Mysteries.

The Sleuths at the Spa epub copy is an exclusive benefit to newsletter readers of Author Vikki Walton. Grab it here.

https://dl.bookfunnel.com/yw0z22wg0g

About the Author

Vikki Walton has always been in love with the mystery genre. As a young girl, she devoured the Nancy Drew books, and later, the mysteries by the Queen of crime, Agatha Christie. Even though she'd been writing for many years, it wasn't until her daughter had to write a novel for her English class that it prompted Vikki to sit down and write her first cozy mystery, Chicken Culprit. Vikki based it on her own life at the time as a suburban homesteader or backyard farmer. While she no longer has chickens or bees, she still enjoys her garden.

While Vikki lives in the beautiful state of Colorado, Carolan Springs is alas, not a real place. Many readers of Vikki's books often comment that they want to visit the small town in the mountains. While not real, it's a conglomerate of many towns and cities found throughout Colorado that are similar to Carolan Springs. As for the name, there are a lot of "Springs" in Colorado, hence the name of the town.

In addition to her best-selling Backyard Farming series, Vikki also has a series set in Texas and one that spans the globe. Christie Taylor is the main character of the Taylor Texas series and is a pie-baking, horse-riding amateur sleuth, while Viviane Masters is a sassy sixty-year-old who travels the globe as a pet and house sitter.

Besides writing cozies, Vikki also writes nonfiction and is an indie author coach, helping other writers who are starting their journey to self-publication. She also writes historical women's fiction under a pen name which focuses on strong women overcoming circumstances in their lives.

Aside from her writing, Vikki enjoys spending time outdoors on the Colorado trails, tending to her garden, or traveling to destinations around the world.

Her books can be found at your favorite retailer and through your local library. If they aren't in stock, simply put in a request for the library to carry her books.